Also by Claire Savage

Magical Masquerade

Phantom Phantasia

Underneath the Tree: 12 Christmas stories from writers in Northern Ireland (Co-edited with Kelly Creighton)

L0 For adults!

The Story

Forest

CLAIRE SAVAGE

Claire Savage

To George,
I hope you enjoy reading
about Freddie's adventures!
Claire

Feb 2021

First published in 2021 by Kindle Direct Publishing (KDP)

A CIP catalogue record for this book
is available from the British Library.

ISBN: 979-8-6868-6258-6

www.clairesavagewriting.wordpress.com

Facebook: Claire Savage - Author

Twitter: @ClaireLSavage

Instagram: clairesavage_editorial

Cover design by Design for Writers

For my nephews – Christos, Alex and Theodor.

And Reuben, who's always at my side.

Contents

The Story Forest

Chapter One

The Extraordinary Monday

There was really nothing to suggest that Monday, January 7 was going to be an extraordinary day. After all, it was the first day back at school after Christmas. January was a dark and dreary month – dark when you awoke and dark when you got home. As for Mondays, well, *everyone* knew that Mondays were the absolute worst days of the week. Even more so when they appeared in January, after the Christmas holidays.

So, far from expecting this particular Monday to be a good day, Freddie had every expectation that it would not. Mondays were so universally disliked there were even *songs* about them. Freddie's mum often sang lines from a song called, *'I Don't Like Mondays'*, to tease him when he muttered about this most woeful day of the week. Granted, his birthday occasionally fell on a Monday, but it was still a school day, so it couldn't really redeem itself at all in Freddie's opinion.

Today's mournful Monday – a so far unremarkable day – was, however, almost over. Freddie was trudging to the library and in a couple of hours would be back at home, where he could start counting down the days to the weekend. School wasn't that bad – if you didn't count homework – but weekends were the absolute best.

Freddie waited as the door of the library opened automatically, bidding him entry inch by inch as if it too hated Mondays and could barely muster movement. When there was enough room for an 11-year-old boy to slip through, Freddie ducked around the heavy door, welcoming the wave of warmth that swept over him.

He waved at his mum behind the desk as he made his way to the usual spot – a small table in a corner at the back of the library surrounded by bookcases and usually private enough that no one bothered him.

Today, however, he was annoyed to find someone sitting in his seat. At *his* table. Freddie stopped mid-step and the man who had invaded his space looked up. The table was covered in sheets of paper and the man, having obviously decided Freddie wasn't worth his attention, returned to reading and jotting down notes.

Freddie smothered a sigh and found another table, where he dumped his schoolbag before seeking out his mum. He spotted her distinctive black curls behind a bookcase in non-fiction. Her librarian ears must have sensed his approach as she turned round to greet him before he had time to breach the silence.

"What's wrong, Fred?"

"There's a *man* at my table," hissed Freddie, trying to keep his voice at an acceptable library level but, as usual, somehow seeming to amplify it with his whispers.

"Shush!" said his mum, flicking her head round to see if anyone had heard him. "You can just sit somewhere else today. It's not especially reserved for you, you know." She raised her eyebrows at her son in amusement.

"I know that!" mumbled Freddie. "But who *is* he? He doesn't look like someone who uses libraries a lot." He thought for a moment. "Too official. Like a teacher, or, or —"

"An inspector from the board of the Library Administration Body," sighed his mum. "Come to inspect our library, I'm afraid. Oh," her eyes brightened. "It looks like he's leaving. You can grab your table now Fred, if you like. Get started on your homework."

"Great," muttered Freddie.

The man had taken brisk steps towards them, however, trapping mother and son before Freddie could escape.

"Ah, Mrs May! Is this your son?" The inspector was a tall weed of a man with glasses and a long hooked nose that protruded over a thin-lipped mouth. He flashed Freddie's mum a smile which failed to reach his eyes, then focused it on Freddie.

"Yes, Mr Tipett; this is Freddie."

"He doesn't look much like you." Mr Tipett narrowed his eyes, as if Freddie was somehow trying to deceive him.

"Takes after his dad with his hair colouring," said Freddie's mum. "But he has my eyes. Redheads usually have blue eyes, you see, not brown."

"If you say so." The inspector seemed to have lost all interest in Freddie. Freddie glowered at him as his mum shooed him away. "Now. About my report …"

"Perhaps we'd better go into my office," his mum said, as Freddie snatched up his bag and hurried over to his usual place. The seat was unpleasantly warm from where Mr Tipett had been sitting and Freddie scowled. So far, there was nothing much he liked about that man.

***

Mr Tipett left the library with the taste of victory on his tongue. It was even better than he'd expected – or worse, depending on which side you were on. And there *were* sides to be chosen, though he knew *his* was the right one.

He sighed with pleasure. Using his role as a local councillor to become a board member of the Library Administration Body, or 'LAB' as most people called it, had been a spectacularly brilliant idea of his. It would make it so much easier to close down these wretched public libraries when he was part of the decision-making team. He'd done a good job so far in getting the inspection of Portsteven Library approved. Now all he had to do was make sure he achieved his goal of getting rid of it.

He squeezed some hand cleanser from a tube he kept in the car and rubbed it into his skin with vigour. You never knew what you might pick up in a place like that, where anyone could just walk in off the street and smear germs over surfaces. Mr Tipett shuddered. He couldn't wait to get back to his nice clean councillor's office with its view of the river – well away from members of the public, up on the fourth floor. Cleanliness and efficiency were what mattered in Mr Tipett's world and libraries had no place in it.

***

Freddie's mum was uncharacteristically quiet as she tidied up the library before they went home. Mr Tipett was long gone but he seemed to have taken some of the head librarian's spark with him.

Normally, at this point in the evening, Freddie tried to hurry her up, but he sensed tonight that something was wrong and so, he didn't grumble when she asked him to tidy the children's reading area and he didn't strike up his usual refrain of, 'Is it time to go yet?'

Besides, something felt a bit 'off' in the library that

evening. Freddie couldn't put his finger on it, but there was definitely something strange in the air. He kept feeling as if someone was watching him, but he could see his mum through the window of her office and he knew that all members of the public had left at five o'clock, as it was early closing that night.

He scooped up the last couple of books from the reading table and put them on the shelf. As he turned to go, something thudded to the ground. It broke the silence like a stone. Freddie jumped.

He spun round and saw a book lying on the floor. It was one that he'd just returned to the shelf a moment ago. He looked at it in annoyance then picked it up and rammed it securely back into the space it had just vacated. There was no chance of it falling again now.

And yet.

As soon as he turned to leave, Freddie heard another loud thump and there the book was again on the floor.

Slightly spooked now, he decided to just leave it where it was. He grabbed his schoolbag and hurried towards the front desk. He was halfway there when something whistled through the air behind him. Sensing it just in time, Freddie whirled around, only just managing to move his head as a book clipped his ear, narrowly avoiding a full-on collision with his face.

"Who threw that?" he yelled, rubbing his throbbing ear.

In her office, his mum gave him a quizzical look as she spoke to someone on the phone.

"There's definitely somebody in here," muttered Freddie, reaching down to retrieve the book. It had fallen open at two blank pages, which he thought was odd. As he picked it up, however, words danced across the page, as if someone invisible was writing into the book.

"What the—?" said Freddie, more curious now then annoyed. His eyes widened as he read the book's message. Scrawled across the pages, over and over, the same phrase was repeated:

'Save our library, Freddie. Save our library, Freddie. Save our library, Freddie.'

Chapter Two

Secrets and Questions

Freddie's mum was more like herself again on the drive home and she hummed as she usually did, in between asking him about his day. Freddie decided not to mention the mysterious message just yet. Besides, the book had reverted to its original text straight after he'd read it and he was beginning to wonder if perhaps he'd imagined it all.

So, he stared out of the window as rain lashed against the pane, answering his mother's questions as he watched the sea smash frothy waves against the lower promenade. Then they passed the harbour and the sea disappeared from view as they turned off for the narrow country road that led home. It was too far from town for Freddie to walk every day, which was why he always went to the library after school; plus his mum preferred to keep an eye on him and make sure he did his homework.

His dad had a job in the city, so he was always home a little later, unless there was a last-minute breaking news story. As a busy newspaper editor, Freddie's dad was often held up by unplanned-for stories across the country. With his mum a librarian and his dad a journalist, it was somewhat unfortunate for Freddie's parents that their son didn't seem to have inherited their love of words.

As they swung into the small driveway at the end of their lane, however, Freddie saw his dad's car parked in its usual spot.

"Great, your dad's home early. Slow time of year for news," said his mum, flashing Freddie a grin. "Run along to your room and get changed, Fred. I want to have a quick chat with your father in private before we have dinner."

Considering Freddie always got changed out of his school uniform as soon as he got home, he wasn't sure why his mum was reminding him, but he supposed she didn't want him hurrying back and barging into her private chat. Which was why he tip-toed very quietly down the hallway and listened carefully outside the kitchen door after flinging off his school things and yanking on a pair of jeans and a jumper.

"… might close us down," he heard his mum say in a voice thin as slate.

"Do you really think they will?" said his dad. He sounded worried.

"Well, the LAB inspector's visit could have gone better. He didn't discuss the full report, said there's still more information to come, but he certainly didn't sound optimistic. They're closing down so many libraries these days, Martin. I'll just have to do my best to make sure that *ours* stays open."

"Don't worry, Merc. I'm sure it'll all work out. You're doing a great job as head librarian. And it's a busier library than most, surely!"

"Yes, it is." Freddie's mum paused. "Which is why I don't see how Mr Tipett's report could be in any way negative, but being busy might not be enough to save us."

"Hmm, yes, it's all about cuts, isn't it? And it's usually the resources our community really needs which get the chop," said Freddie's dad. "Just stay on your guard, Merc, and keep me updated on what's happening with it all. I'll help any way that I can."

Freddie moved away as his mum's footsteps approached the door. Close the library? If they did that then his mum and others would lose their jobs. Lots of people used the library every day, for all sorts of things – reading of course, but also, using the computers. They had kids' groups too and ran courses for older people – the 'Silver Surfers' his mum liked to call them. Freddie had seen people writing in the library too - maybe novelists – and he did his homework there. Why on earth would they close it?

True, it could do with a bit of an update, but paint didn't cost much, did it? His skin grew clammy as another thought came to him. If the library closed, maybe they'd have to move to the city. His dad often complained about his daily commute and how much handier it would be if they only lived closer to his office.

As Freddie pulled on his trainers, back in his bedroom, his thoughts flitted to the mysterious message in the book: *'Save our library, Freddie.'* Apparently someone else was worried about his mum's library and Freddie was determined to find out who.

***

By the time Freddie was called for dinner, his mum seemed to have shaken off her worry and was singing snatches of songs from her favourite band, Queen, as she dished up with his dad. It was no coincidence that she had named her son Freddie, after the band's deceased vocalist, though Freddie knew his mum might have preferred it had he been born with a dark mop like that of her and her musical hero, rather than springing from the womb with a shock of red hair which only seemed to brighten the older he got.

His dad liked to tease his wife about how the dominant 'ginger genes' had won out, though always with a smile on his face, as Freddie knew he found his wife's obsession endearing. He must do, anyway, Freddie realised, after he discovered his mum had actually changed her name legally ("Just like Freddie Mercury himself!") from Catherine to Mercury years ago. The fact that their surname was May was the icing on the cake, as the Queen guitarist was called Brian May. So, Mercury was very happy indeed that her son, while looking nothing in the slightest like Freddie Mercury, shared his initials and first name, if not his features and aptitude for music.

"If only you'd be born with a few extra teeth in your head, then you might have become a singing protégé too!" his mother had told him brightly, when he was younger. "Oh well, Fred. We can't have everything! But don't worry, I still love you!"

Freddie's mum was a little different from other mothers, but just like his dad, Freddie found that her eccentricities only made him love her more.

"All right, Fred?" she asked him now, as she set his plate down in front of him. "You look a bit lost in thought."

"Just, er, thinking about school," said Freddie quickly. "I thought I might get involved with the radio this year. They let us do interviews and stuff. Just like you, dad. Might be fun."

His father raised his eyebrows at Mercury. "Indeed! Well, well. We'll make a journalist out of you yet, Fred." He looked rather pleased about that and spent the rest of the meal telling Freddie all about what it took to be a good reporter and the best kind of questions to ask interviewees. Freddie tried to concentrate on what his dad was saying, but his mind couldn't help but wander back to the library and the self-writing book. He certainly had some questions he wanted to ask, but to whom would he be directing them to?

Chapter Three

Knock, Knock

His local town library might be under threat, but Freddie had another library which he spent time in during the week. The school library. The principal of Portsteven Primary School always took great pleasure in reminding his pupils they had been very fortunate indeed to have "secured funding from the public purse" before the cuts came. As a result, they were in the rather privileged position of being a primary school in possession of both a separate library and an in-house radio station, with speakers fitted in every classroom, as well as the assembly hall, so broadcasts could be enjoyed by everyone in the school.

Freddie, however, was no bookworm.

It wasn't that he didn't *like* books, he just never

wanted to sit still long enough to read one.

"You're missing out on all sorts of marvellous adventures, Fred," his mum often told him, but she seemed hopeful that he would find his way into books at some stage and so didn't try to force them on him, other than making sure he read what was required for school. She did, however, always include a book with his birthday and Christmas presents.

Tuesday afternoon was library time for Freddie's class. He also decided it was the perfect time to tell his friends about what had happened yesterday.

"Brain," he whispered, as the class milled about the shelves for fresh reading material. "You know how you like books?"

Brian – or 'Brain' as his friends called him, owing to his general 'know-it-all-ness' – gave Freddie a quizzical look. "Yeah, so?"

"Well ..." Freddie paused. "Well, have you ever seen, like, a *message* written in one?"

Brain's eyes narrowed suspiciously behind his glasses. The lenses to correct his long-sightedness magnified his eyes, giving him an owl-like appearance. He was always fiddling with them and he did so now, adjusting the slightly crooked frames as he scrutinised his friend. "Are you having me on, Fred? Of *course* I see messages in books. That's sort of the point of them!"

"What? Oh, yeah, very funny," said Freddie. "I don't mean general *words*, Brain." He really felt that he wasn't explaining himself very well. "I mean – have you ever seen a book go blank and then, like, write a message to you in front of your eyes?"

Brain was looking at him as if he'd just grown another head. "Er, no, Fred." He laughed nervously. "You sure you're feeling alright?"

"No, wait, you don't understand," hissed Freddie. They'd caught the attention of their teacher, however, so there was no chance for further conversation until after school. By that stage their other friend, Rob, was pestering them about why they'd been told off in the library, so Freddie explained everything about the previous day to them both as they left school.

"I don't know, Fred," said Rob, scratching his messy blond hair. "Sounds kinda weird to me. Sure you didn't imagine it? Sure you're not going loopy?" He grinned.

Freddie shoved him good-humouredly, almost toppling his wiry friend, who was slim as a toothpick despite the hours he spent trying to beef up in his karate lessons. "*No*, I'm not going *loopy*, thanks Rob," he said, as Brain wound his finger against the side of his head. "At least, I don't think so." He frowned. "Come to the library with me and see for yourselves. I want to see if it happens again and find out who wrote that message."

"Can't. Mum's picking me up," said Rob.

"Yeah, my gran's getting me," said Brain. "But we can come tomorrow. Just be careful you don't get caught talking to yourself this afternoon!"

"Ha ha," said Freddie. He waved at his friends as they headed for the main entrance of the school. Portsteven Primary School was contained within the grounds of Portsteven College, which was surrounded by a tall pebble-dash wall. The front gates opened onto the road which led into town, the entrance most of the pupils used to come and go. There was also a back entry, however, which was the one Freddie now headed towards.

The back of Portsteven's schools was, in Freddie's and most of the other pupils' opinions, infinitely more interesting than the front because it opened onto a cliff path, also known as The Nun's Walk. Freddie knew of

19

no other school which had ever been a nunnery in a previous life – and one with a supposed ghost to boot. The Nun's Walk led, eventually, to the beach if you headed left and offered a shortcut to the town – and the library – if you chose right, which Freddie now did. He hurried along the winding path, glancing at the waves churning at the base of the cliff before he clattered down the steps which led to the promenade.

As the library came into view his heart quickened. He'd soon find out if he'd been imagining things.

***

By the time it came to tidy up in the library that evening, Freddie had convinced himself that he must have been mistaken about yesterday's incident after all. Whoever had heard of a book writing secret messages to people anyway – especially people who didn't even particularly *like* reading?

As a result, he'd more or less abandoned his plan and wasn't really paying attention as he picked up scattered books and placed them back on the shelves. He was tidying in the non-fiction section when a large volume toppled from the shelf just above his head and slammed onto the floor inches from his feet.

"Hey! That nearly knocked me out! Who's there?"

Freddie ran to the other side of the bookcase but, of course, there was nobody there. The library was empty. Besides, with it being an old library, the bookcases had heavy wooden frames with strong backs, so there was no possibility of books being pushed through solid wood from the other side.

Freddie froze as he heard what sounded like laughter coming from the bookcase. Maybe he really *was* going loopy, like Rob had joked. Despite his reservations, however, he whispered, "Who's there?"

All was quiet.

A brisk *knock, knock* made Freddie jump.

He waited, heart hammering as he held his breath without even realising it. Nothing happened for a few seconds and then, the sound repeated. Someone was knocking on the bookcase, a steady *'tap, tap, tap'*. It sounded as though it was coming from somewhere lower down.

Freddie crouched beside the end of the bookcase, feeling only a little stupid, as the knocking continued.

His breath had quickened now and his fingers trembled a little as he felt along the wood.

"Where *are* you?" he muttered. "*Who* are you?"

He knocked on the wood himself to see if anything would happen. Someone giggled and Freddie gulped. It sounded as if whoever it was, was *inside* the bookcase, which he knew was absolutely impossible and out of the question. Just *what* was going on? It couldn't be mice, could it? Did mice giggle?

"No, of course they don't!" he said to himself sharply. "It must be some sort of trick. Maybe some kid left behind one of those stupid books that makes animal noises. Yeah, that must be it. Why didn't I think of that before?"

Freddie let out a ragged breath of relief. He'd almost believed in something completely unbelievable for a moment. And yet …

The knocking and giggling had stopped, only to be replaced by a sawing sound. Still crouched by the end of the bookcase, Freddie saw a thin black line appear on the wood, curving up from the floor in the shape of an arch. He narrowed his eyes as what looked like a small round handle appeared to one side of what now looked remarkably like a tiny door. A door which, as Freddie stared in surprise, opened inwards just a crack.

Chapter Four

A Darkening of Door

Trembling with anticipation, Freddie placed his fingers on the little door and gave it a gentle push. He half-expected it to disappear or, failing that, to stand firm, but to his surprise and immense excitement, it opened obligingly inwards some more.

All Freddie could see was inky darkness but he swallowed his disappointment and tentatively poked his fingers into the small space, which was about the size of a mouse hole. The air felt cooler inside the bookcase and Freddie waggled his fingers around a little, feeling for anything which might lie hidden in this secret hidey-hole.

He thought for a moment that he'd brushed against

something warm, but was distracted by footsteps behind him. Immediately, he snatched his hand back and pulled the little door towards him. It closed with a quiet click, the outline sinking back into the varnished old wood of the bookcase, leaving it completely ordinary-looking once again.

Freddie's mum was a very open-minded sort of person but he wanted to keep this to himself for now. Besides, the door had disappeared so even Mercury would find it difficult to believe he wasn't making things up. Adults, thought Freddie, always seemed to want proof and evidence before they believed things.

"Hard facts, Fred," as his dad liked to remind him, when talking about his newspaper. "A good journalist will only ever write an article rooted in solid evidence and backed up by reliable sources. You must always be able to stand by your story, remember that!"

Freddie would certainly stand by *this* story, but until he had more facts about what had just happened, he felt fully justified in keeping his secret. He had a feeling, however, that the library was about to get a lot more interesting.

"Fred! What on earth are you doing down there?"

Freddie leapt to his feet and flashed his mum a grin. "Thought I saw a pound coin," he said.

"And?"

"Er, turns out it was just wishful thinking."

"Hmm," his mum gave him an amused look. "Wishful thinking indeed, Fred. I hope you haven't spent all your pocket money already? Though I'm sure I could find you some more jobs to do if you wanted —"

"No thanks, mum!" said Freddie quickly. More chores was the last thing he wanted, especially when there were mysterious doors to investigate and much-needed conversations to be had with Brain and Rob. "I'm good, thanks."

"Yes, well, it's time we were getting home," said Mercury. "Come on, grab your schoolbag. I'm all cleared up."

Freddie thought his mum looked a bit more tired than she had yesterday and he wondered if she was still worried about Mr Tipett and his library inspection. He also wondered what Mr Tipett would say if he knew there was a strange little door which seemed to be able to appear and disappear at will at the bottom of one of the bookcases.

As Freddie swung his bag onto his shoulder and followed his mum out to the car, he thought it really was amazing the things a day could reveal – if you only took the time to stop and look.

***

At break-time the next day, Freddie filled his friends in on the mysterious miniature door in the bookcase. Rob's eyebrows shot up into his hair, while Brain listened, deep in thought.

"Sounds a bit far-fetched to me," said Rob. "In fact, stuff that, it sounds absolutely bonkers, Fred! Doors don't just appear! Especially not wee magic ones at the bottom of library bookcases. Not that I've ever *looked* for them, right enough …"

"I'm not making it up," said Freddie. "Why would I, when I know how weird it sounds? I wouldn't believe it either, except - *I've* seen it."

"And the message in the book," said Brain. "It really asked you to help save the library?"

"Yeah. So, what do you think?"

"Well, it certainly looks as though someone wants

27

your attention, Fred," said Brain slowly.

"They have it!"

"So … I think you just need them to make themselves known to you, somehow."

"Hold on a minute," said Rob. "Are you saying what I think you're saying?"

Brain's mouth twitched up at the corners. "Depends what you think we're saying."

"I *mean*," said Rob, "are we talking as if this is real? As if there are, like, I don't know," he leaned forward and whispered, "*little* people. Like, *fairies*?"

"Possibly," said Brain matter-of-factly.

"Are you actually mad?!" said Rob.

"Well, I mean, it might not be actual *fairies*," said Freddie. He cast a sidelong look at Brain. "Right?"

"Well, I don't know, Fred. You're the one talking about personal messages appearing as if by magic in books, and doors materialising on bookcases. If it's not all in your head …" Freddie glared at Brain, so he added hurriedly, "What else could it be?"

"I don't know," muttered Freddie, wishing now that he hadn't mentioned any of this to his friends at all.

Rob was watching the pair of them with a horrified

look on his face. "This *cannot* get out," he said. "If anyone hears us saying we've seen fairies we'll be a laughing stock! No one sees fairies. Well, maybe girls like to *think* they can …" He frowned.

"Seeing fairies isn't just a girl thing," hissed Freddie. "Why would it be? There's bound to be boy fairies too!"

"I give you Master Frodo and his quest, for one example of that," piped up Brain. He rolled his eyes at the blank looks on Freddie and Rob's faces.

"Anyway," continued Freddie. "We don't know *what* it is at the library. It might be something else entirely."

Rob didn't look convinced but by the time the bell had called them back inside, he had at least agreed to visit the library after school with Freddie and Brain the following day. Brain couldn't make it today after all and Rob said he'd rather they all went together, though Freddie suspected he was just trying to put off the visit in case of what they might find.

That left Freddie one more evening alone to find out what they were dealing with. He wasn't sure about Brain's fairy theory but one thing was certain. There was definitely something strange going on at Portsteven Library and it couldn't be a coincidence that all this was happening just as the library was under threat.

***

Freddie kept a vigil by the bookcase all evening but was disappointed when his mum called him to go home and nothing had happened. He'd watched the shelves like a hawk and had even tried tapping at the base of the side panel, in the hope that the door might appear again, but it was all to no avail.

It wasn't until he was packing up his schoolbag that he saw the note sticking out of his English exercise book. He grabbed it immediately but just at that moment his mum appeared, so he stuffed it into his pocket.

"Come on, Fred," said Mercury, tapping her watch. "Time's ticking on."

"I'm ready." Freddie threw the rest of his things into his bag and followed his mum. The note just *had* to be from the mystery person and he was itching to see what it said.

Chapter Five

Midnight Meeting

As soon as he got home, Freddie raced to his bedroom and opened the crumpled note with trembling hands.

It read: *'Meet me at your house library at midnight – M.'*

Freddie read the tiny handwriting again. 'House library'? They must mean the study, which he supposed *was* more like a library, really. It had a table and a computer but was mostly full of books, crammed onto a couple of old mahogany bookcases his mum had found in a second-hand shop. They scraped the ceiling and were filled top-to-toe with tomes of all kinds.

His dad was working late at the paper tonight, so it was just Freddie and his mum for dinner. He hoped his midnight meeting wouldn't be disturbed by his dad coming home – because, of course, Freddie was definitely going to find out who had summoned him – but he knew that it could be 1am before his dad got back, so he should be safe enough.

Normally, Freddie chatted with his mum about school or she told him funny stories from the library, like people asking her to locate 'that book with the blue cover' they really wanted to read, or about the strange things others left behind, which ended up in the Lost and Found box. Mercury had a talent for storytelling and always made Freddie laugh with her facial expressions and eye-rolling, but tonight she seemed to have as much on her mind as her son and the conversation was much diluted.

"Mum," said Freddie as he tucked into his dessert of apple crumble and custard, "I was just wondering if Mr Tipett had been back to the library? You know, the tall man with the glasses?"

Mercury sighed. "Oh, I know who you mean, Fred. I'm glad to say that, no, Mr Tipett has not been back, but I've spoken to him on the phone. He's yet to deliver his full report on the library but," she paused. "I might as well tell you, Freddie. I think the LAB is trying to close us down."

"But why?" said Freddie, his spoon midway to his mouth. "You work really hard, mum, and loads of people use the library. Can't they see that? Why would they want to close somewhere that so many people use?"

Mercury smiled. "Yes, Fred, but I'm afraid that when people in decision-making roles decide on something like this they usually have the power – or find the means – to get their way. We *are* a busy library and I've already got a petition going, which lots of people have signed, but I'm not sure if we'll be able to convince them to let us stay open if they're hard set on shutting the place down. It really could do with a makeover too, which doesn't help our case." She frowned. "Though I personally like its lived-in décor. But it costs a lot of money for a refurb and it's very unlikely the 'Powers That Be' will want to spend it!"

"So, if it was more state-of-the-art it would be harder to shut down?" asked Freddie.

His mum smiled. "Well, it would certainly help our case, love, but again, I'm not sure if it would save us. Anyway, there's no need for you to worry about all this stuff; leave that to me and your dad. I've got Laurel on the case too. She's keen to have a peaceful protest, with placards and everything, if it comes to it."

Laurel was Mercury's best friend and was like a favourite aunt to Freddie. Like his mum, she was a big bookworm, though she preferred self-help and self-improvement books to fiction. She did, however, have a penchant for poetry and while she wasn't quite such a big Queen fan as Mercury, appreciated the band's lyrical compositions.

"We'll make a poet out of you yet, young Freddie," she often said, though in her case it was with an extra twinkle in her eye, as she knew it wound Freddie up and she liked to keep him going about it. "Your namesake was a great lyricist as well as a singer!"

In truth, Freddie thought the lead singer of Queen *had* been kind of impressive. He'd watch videos online and thought he was a bit of a joker, which he liked. He also had to admit that his voice was sort of amazing. Unfortunately, the young red-haired boy named after him didn't have a musical bone in his body and didn't think he ever would.

He helped his mum clear the table and then spent the rest of the evening counting down the hours till bedtime, which *definitely* wasn't like him. At last, he said goodnight to his mum and settled into bed, willing the clock towards midnight. He'd set his alarm too, wrapped up in a jumper beside his pillow, just in case.

***

Freddie woke to a buzzing by his ear. It took him a minute to remember he'd hidden his alarm clock inside his jumper, to muffle the sound. And a good job too, as he must have fallen asleep after all.

Carefully, he crept out of his bedroom, pausing at the door to check for parental movements before tip-toeing out onto the landing. The coast seemed clear. His mum must be in bed and his dad not yet home, as a quick glance out the window showed only his mum's car in the drive.

The study, or book room, as Freddie thought of it, was at the other end of the landing, past the bathroom at the top of the stairs and his parents' room. The door was ajar and creaked only a little as Freddie pushed it open. Why, he wondered, did everything seem to be noisier at night? He pulled the door to behind him and only then switched on his pocket torch, keeping the beam low. On his right was the desk where his parents did any work they needed to do, with shelves lining the walls behind it. The main bookcases, however, were opposite, on Freddie's left, and it was to these that he made his way.

It was a few minutes past midnight and Freddie hoped he hadn't missed the mysterious 'M', whoever that might be. He wasn't sure what he was supposed to do exactly, so he sat down on the floor in between the two bookcases and waited.

He nearly jumped out of his pyjamas when a voice said, "Well, it's about time. *You're* late!"

Chapter Six

A Kind of Magic

"Who's there?" said Freddie, his heart racing. He knew he'd come to meet someone, but still, it was a little bit disconcerting when a voice spoke out of the darkness at you from a bookcase.

A tap on wood sounded to his right.

"Over here."

It sounded like a female and as Freddie looked where the voice had directed him, he saw he was correct.

A young girl, maybe about his own age, was sitting on a shelf just about level with Freddie's head, legs swinging in the air. She wore an amused expression and was studying him just as intently as he was her. She had big pale eyes and a messy bob, which she shook back from her face.

"Hello, Freddie. I'm Meg." She stuck out her hand for Freddie to shake and they both laughed as he reached up and grasped it somewhat awkwardly between his finger and thumb.

"If you agree to help then we can operate more on the same level," said Meg. "You've come tonight, so I assume you're willing?" She raised her brows in question.

"Help with what, exactly?" said Freddie. "Oh, OK, I know, with the library," he said, as Meg rolled her eyes and muttered "Keep up." He flushed and was glad of the darkness around them. "But *how* can I help and, well, who *are* you?"

Meg grinned. "Well, it's really easier to *show* you who I – *we* – are," she said. "Will you help us, then? If you say yes then I can explain everything. Answers will be earned only if I know I can trust you and they're better shared somewhere more private."

Freddie was really no further forward about anything that was happening, but his curiosity won out over his common sense and he simply nodded. Anyway, maybe he was dreaming. He used to sleepwalk when he was little. Although he did indeed appear to be talking with a book-sized girl on a bookshelf in the dark, maybe he was actually still asleep in bed.

"Excellent!" said Meg. "Now, come a little closer and I'll get you ready."

"Um, ready for what?"

"For travelling, of course. Don't worry – it's quite safe."

Freddie rose warily onto his knees so he was eye-level with Meg. She muttered a string of strange words and then, before he realised what was happening, blew coloured dust into his face. Freddie's eyes watered and he sneezed as some of the powder went up his nose. He didn't have time to dwell on the slight discomfort, however, because the next thing he knew, the bookshelves were whizzing past him and then towering above him. Freddie felt a bit queasy, as if he'd just travelled in a very fast lift. One minute he'd been eye-to-eye with a Meg whom he could have carried in his hand, the next he was eye-to-eye with a Meg more or less his own height.

"How ... How did you do that?" He gaped. "*What*

did you do?"

Meg grinned at him again. "Do what?" she said mischievously. "Shrink you or get down here super-fast to greet you?"

"Well, both!" Freddie looked up at the bookcase. It looked as tall to him now as Big Ben.

"Well … you might not believe me," teased Meg.

"Try me."

She winked and tapped her nose. "It's a kind of magic, Freddie. Now, come on – let's go!"

***

Meg grabbed Freddie's hand and pulled him through a tiny door which appeared at the base of the bookcase after she tapped it and muttered more words that Freddie had never heard before. He had no choice but to follow her in. The door sealed behind them.

"Now," said Meg in a louder voice. "We can speak freely in here. No need to whisper, Freddie! No one can hear you now except for you, me and the rest of the Book-Keepers, if any are about, which I don't think they are right now."

"Yeah, said the kidnapper to their victim," said Freddie, giving a nervous laugh.

"Ha! You're funny," said Meg, dragging him down what was so far a well-lit, but empty, tunnel. She glanced at him. "You *are* joking though, right? I mean, you came of your own free will and I'm hardly a kidnapper or an axe-murderer." She grinned. "Though I don't suppose I'd tell you if I was."

"Very funny," said Freddie, but he felt better. "Um, who or what, are Book-Keepers?"

"Ah, now you're asking! Good question. I can't tell you everything about Book-Keepers as I'm not sure even *we* know all the ins and outs of our history, *but*, all you really need to know is that I'm a Book-Keeper and everyone else down here is a Book-Keeper. As long as books have existed, so have we, and our job is to protect them, care for them, find them eager readers and keep their stories alive.

"We live all over the world and you can only access the Book-Keeper community through doors like the one we just entered. Well, mostly." She tapped her nose secretively.

"Bookcase doors?"

"Exactly. Any bookcase, anywhere. Wooden, metal or any other material besides. Though we do love a good old wooden bookcase." She sighed. "Wood carries its own stories, you see, and is infinitely more interesting than plastic, for example." She shuddered. "Anyway, that's the Cliff Notes. Questions?"

"Uh, only about a *million*," said Freddie. His mind was in overdrive. "Can you travel anywhere in the world through your tunnels then?"

"Yep. We could swing by a library in Italy or Switzerland or Russia right now. But we won't. Got other things to do."

"Brilliant," was all Freddie could really say to that. His attention was diverted by his surroundings, as the tunnel was no longer bare-walled. Windows had appeared on either side of him and he caught glimpses of figures behind them. "Er, are we still in the bookcase, somehow?"

"Of course not. The doors just connect our network of tunnels. When you enter a bookcase door the tunnel *begins* in the bookcase but then acts as a sort of portal, I suppose, to our world. Don't worry – we're not living in your walls, Freddie! Anyway, we're here now. There are faster ways of travelling but I thought it would help you if we took it slow for your first trip."

They had reached what appeared to be more solid wood but, once again, Meg tapped it, said some strange words and another door appeared. They stepped through.

Chapter Seven

The Travelling Tree

The door opened between thick stumps of wood, which Freddie quickly realised were the beginnings of roots. He stepped back to take a better look and saw that it was one of many doors cut into the trunk of a simply enormous tree, which was so tall, he couldn't see the top. The trunk's girth was at least as thick as a house, if not two. Freddie watched in amazement as his and Meg's door faded from view. Some of the others did too, though not all of them.

"We travel to so many places that it would be impossible even for the Travelling Tree to accommodate every door," explained Meg. "Some of the doors *are* permanent, though. They lead to the most famous libraries in the world. Anyway, welcome to Thesaurus." She swept her arms wide and grinned.

The Travelling Tree was, quite simply, enormous and Freddie just couldn't stop staring at it, so much so that he felt a crick develop in his neck. He wondered how many people it would take to encircle its huge girth and how many buildings tall it reached upwards. It certainly surpassed any sky-scraper he'd seen back home. Their door had been right at the bottom of the trunk, but others were cut into the timber in all sorts of places and in all sizes and shapes. The wood itself was gnarled and knotted, covered in lumps and bumps, fissures and wider cracks. It was mottled with moss and lichen, imprinted with many different kinds of life other than its own.

Freddie was fascinated. He felt he could look at it all day and still only uncover a fraction of what this magnificent tree was. The first branches began quite a way up and as he squinted at the tree's odd-shaped leaves he gave a start.

"Are those *books*?" he asked Meg.

"Yep, what else?" She gave him a quizzical look.

The books hung downwards from their spines, pages rustling in the breeze so they looked like restless birds. It seemed almost as if the Travelling Tree was talking to them and perhaps it was. Freddie knew from his science work at school that even in his own world, trees communicated through their labyrinthine root systems – what more could they achieve here, he wondered, where they grew their own reading material?

The Travelling Tree was located in what looked like a town square, with all the hustle and bustle of the Book-Keeper community taking place around it.

"It's amazing," said Freddie. "Is it one of a kind?"

"No, each Book-Keeper community has its own Travelling Tree, though none are alike. They vary in size too. Our town is quite big so we have a larger tree to accommodate our needs; other communities may be smaller so will have a smaller tree to suit them. Anyway, follow me. I want to show you something."

***

Meg pulled Freddie after her and the Travelling Tree watched them go. It was rare that anyone other than a Book-Keeper journeyed through its chambers, so it was always nice to welcome fresh blood. Granted, this new boy tasted more of sunshine and soil than the preferred woody, leathery flavours of the bookish, but that didn't mean Meg had chosen wrongly. No, there was adventure and a will for action in her new companion, qualities the Travelling Tree admired and was certain would come in useful. The rest would no doubt develop in time.

The Travelling Tree sighed, its pages rustling. It was connected to all the Travelling Trees around the world and sensed their growing anxiety. More and more libraries were under threat every day; never in their lifetimes had they been in such peril – and they had felt the warmth of countless suns and the cool gaze of many moons. If libraries kept closing, they would lose more than doorways; readers would lose precious access to books and Book-Keepers the ability to protect them and match them to eager eyes.

What's more, where would all the unwanted books go? Who would feed the imaginations and buoy the spirits of those who depended on borrowing books and who couldn't afford to buy their own regular supply? What would the world look like if imagination shrivelled up and shrunk into nothing? If it became nothing more than a fable and the world metamorphosed into one where people lacked the ability to see beyond what was in front of them. And just what would become of the Book-Keepers …?

The Travelling Tree knew something of the hardships people faced and understood that when times were tight, literature became a luxury for the few. Almost every Travelling Tree was sensing similar troubles at the moment. This boy, however, tasted of hope. The Travelling Tree in Thesaurus would watch and wait and listen as his story unfolded.

***

Freddie followed Meg as best he could without tripping, his eyes constantly drawn to one peculiar thing after another. First of all, the buildings all appeared to be built from giant books. One large book sat like a hat upon the tops of the houses, the eaves being the pages. Meanwhile, some had whole books as single walls while others bore the look of bricks which, upon a second glance, Freddie saw were actually lots of smaller books stacked on top of each other.

The windows did appear to be ordinary glass and as

for the people, well, if it hadn't been for the Travelling Tree and the book buildings, Freddie might have believed himself to be hurrying down any street at home. Indeed, he was a little disappointed at how spectacularly ordinary they looked.

The streets were lined with lampposts that looked like pencils, the rubber bit at the top where the light seemed to be. There were bins in the shape of giant pencil sharpeners – Freddie saw a girl drop a wrapper into one – while tall bookmarks wedged into the ground proclaimed what he supposed were street names.

"Hey, where are we going?" he puffed. He hoped his dad didn't decide to check in on him when he got home from work, which he sometimes did. If he popped his head round Freddie's door tonight he'd see an empty bed, as Freddie hadn't thought to stuff it with his pillow. A basic mistake, he knew. Then again, he hadn't planned on travelling through a bookcase with a strange girl to some sort of alternate reality.

"OK, we're here." Meg grinned. "You know," she said to Freddie, giving him a sideways glance. "You seem to be taking all of this awfully well."

"I know," said Freddie, who was surprised himself.

"I think it's because part of me thinks I'm still sleeping. Don't worry, I'm sure I'll freak out plenty later on!" He looked around them. "So, where are we, then?"

Meg smiled. "Somewhere special. Come on."

They were standing outside a large door of heavy oak. Meg had led them through the increasingly twisty streets of the town with great determination and she looked quite pleased with herself. She rapped the door and they waited. After what felt like ages it creaked slowly inwards to admit them. Meg slid through the gap and Freddie decided there was nothing for it but to follow.

Inside, it was dark and quiet and cool, yet Freddie felt a presence. More Book-Keepers? The room made him nervous and he suddenly wondered why on earth he'd come here. Nobody knew where he was, or, he presumed, that he was even missing yet, and there was no *way* they would ever find him here. And now, on top of being in some weird sort of alternate reality, Freddie was inside what felt like a huge chamber filled with darkness and who knew what else.

"Er, Meg, where are you?" he said, reaching out into the blackness around him. "And where are *we*, exactly?"

"You'll see," said Meg.

Freddie *didn't* see and he was starting to get annoyed with his guide. He was just about to ask her to explain herself properly or else take him home, when the chamber began to brighten, as something glowed around them. Freddie started to see the outlines of strange shapes, which didn't exactly make him feel any better, as he still couldn't see what they were. At least they weren't moving.

The glow pulsed stronger and stronger, eating away the darkness until the space was bathed in blinding light. Freddie squeezed his eyes shut against it. Just as he felt that it was getting unbearable, even with closed eyes, the light dimmed again.

"What *is* that?" he hissed.

"That's the Invisible Woman," said Meg.

Chapter Eight

Into the Story Forest

"Um, who, exactly, is the Invisible Woman?" said Freddie. "And more importantly, what does she want with us?"

"She's the one who keeps us all," whispered Meg. "No one's ever seen her, except in the form of light. She mostly exists on another plain but appears in times of need – to warn or to give prophecy."

"Right," said Freddie. "Still confused."

"Shh, she'll show us what we need to know. That's why I brought you here. This is where she normally appears to us. It's a sort of storage facility which everyone shares and it contains almost everything you can think of. I was hoping she'd come and so she has. It's not always obvious what she means at first, but it usually makes sense in the end."

The light had dimmed back down into a softly glowing orb, which appeared to be directing them towards another part of the chamber. Freddie could now see that they were surrounded by bookshelves of all shapes and sizes. What else, he thought. There were also various unusual objects in, around and on them, most of which he couldn't begin to identify.

The Invisible Woman was hovering by a tall ornate mirror and, as Freddie and Meg approached, the orb melted into the glass. Meg stepped through without any hesitation, while Freddie gaped in horror.

"Come on!" she hissed back. Seeing him hesitate, she grabbed Freddie's arm and pulled him through before he had time to stop her.

***

Beyond the mirror, or rather, inside it, was a world even stranger than the one they'd just left behind. Freddie was getting a bit worried about just how many realities they were visiting. He hoped the way back was as simple as the way forward.

The scene before him stopped his thoughts immediately, however, as he drank in everything around him in awe. If he'd thought he was in a dream before, then surely he must be in the heart of one now.

The sky was purple and pink and yellow and two moons hung like lanterns, bathing everything in a silvery glow. A glittering river wound through open countryside, soft music drifting up from the water. Fireflies flashed in the air and the trees were bedecked in leaves of silver and gold, which winked in the double moonlight as they fluttered in the breeze.

Freddie thought it was all very strange and beautiful but he had no idea why this Invisible Woman had brought them here or, indeed, where she had now disappeared to. He shivered and had an overwhelming urge to be snuggled back in his bed, despite all of this beauty around him.

"What now?" he asked Meg.

Meg frowned. "I don't know," she said slowly. "Mirrors lead different people to different places, so I just need to figure out where exactly we are …" Her eyes narrowed and then her face broke into a smile of relief. "Aha! I see the orb, over by those trees … She's taking us to the Story Forest."

"Sorry to keep repeating myself, but the *what*?"

"Come on!" Meg grabbed Freddie's sleeve again and yanked him after her. "You don't want to miss this, trust me."

They raced over to the edge of what Freddie could now see was indeed a thick forest, the orb waiting patiently for them at its periphery. The light throbbed like a beating heart and Freddie wondered what the Invisible Woman's true form was really like. She couldn't be an orb all the time, surely.

Their mysterious guide led them under the cool canopy of clustering trees and Freddie felt a frisson of excitement, all longing for a cosy bed banished from his mind. He didn't know what to expect from a Story Forest, but he had a feeling it was going to be memorable.

***

The Story Forest was wreathed in twilight and moon-glow, silver spearing through the thick canopy of evergreens like enchanted swords. Branches bristled and fistled as Freddie and Meg passed by, bedecked with tiny lights which shimmered and winked at them like stars.

The forest felt alive.

Freddie sensed it breathing around him. He heard whispers where the trees swayed their boughs. The air around him hummed and he could almost taste the magic he felt pulsing at the heart of this bewitching place.

It was cool in the Story Forest, but not unpleasantly so; it was the sort of welcome chill which came after stepping out of the sun and a busy day into the quiet confines of an old stone building. It wrapped around Freddie and made his skin shiver. He felt calm and at peace and, in a strange way, connected to the forest, as if he had become another part of this living organism simply by stepping into it.

"I know," Meg whispered, without Freddie uttering a sound. "It's pretty amazing, isn't it?"

The orb still pulsed up ahead of them and they followed it obediently, threading through the greenery on winding paths patted into shape by fox paws, rabbits' and, perhaps, wondered Freddie, some mythical types of beasts? He had a feeling that anything might be found in the Story Forest.

As they journeyed deeper in, Freddie noticed doors and symbols carved into some of the tree trunks they passed. The trees themselves were now a mixture of species; Freddie spotted ancient oak, beech and hazel amongst the firs and wondered at them all growing together in harmony. Meg noticed him staring.

"Trees talk, you know, and not just here – in your world, too. In the Story Forest, many species co-exist, sharing stories and providing homes to all sorts of tree-dwellers. Their roots grow down into a network of tunnels underground too – a type of labyrinth – hanging like chandeliers and carrying tales from above-ground to the earth-dwellers. Don't worry," she added, sensing Freddie's question, "the earth-dwellers are mostly harmless. There's more than them to be worried about."

"Like, er, wolves, maybe?" asked Freddie.

"You betcha. And Book Worms, witches, goblins, imps and fairies. There's good on all sides, of course, but just as it has its heroes, the Story Forest is also home to villains …"

"Hmm, I was sort of joking," said Freddie, glancing

around him uneasily. "But I suppose where there's good, there's bad."

"And where there's bad, there's good. Exactly. The thing to remember is that in every story (outside of a ready-made book) *you* control the ending and there's *always* a way for 'good' to overcome 'bad'. It can just sometimes take a while, that's all."

"Is that why we're here? Is this some sort of a test? Am I being *tested*? Because I'd really rather someone had warned me about that before I followed you blindly through a bookcase, a Travelling Tree and a magic mirror to a *Story* Forest." Freddie felt his cheeks flush. His former excitement was ebbing away as the forest closed in around them and all this talk of badness and beasts wasn't helping. How dare Meg and this Invisible Woman/orb, who still hadn't even spoken to them, just expect him to be OK with being led into what was seeming to be more and more like a really bad idea? They certainly weren't giving very much away.

"Relax, Freddie. We should be fine. I'm going to take a guess that the Invisible Woman just wants to show you the forest and what's possible within it – and the imagination. You said yourself that you're not a big lover of books, so perhaps she wants to help you understand what we're really trying to save with the library. It's about more than what you might think.

"Anyway, heroes in stories rarely have everything explained to them when they're in the process of becoming heroes. They get the title because they usually end up adventuring and battling evil when they least expect it!"

"Well, as long as I'm sticking to the rules of storytelling …" muttered Freddie, but he had to admit, he felt a little better.

The sarcasm slid off Meg like butter from a hot pan. "Don't grumble, Freddie, or you'll miss all the fun!"

The forest was still mostly quiet but Freddie could hear an undertone of music and singing bubbling through the air. Now and again laughter joined in with the music. It all seemed very far away and yet, it was also as if it was playing right inside Freddie's head.

The trees creaked now and again and Freddie was sure he saw a door close in the trunk of one as they approached it. He felt the unseen gazes of many eyes tickling his skin and yet so far, they had seen no one. A stream chattered alongside them to the left.

"A story stream," said Meg, smiling. "Drink from that and you might find yourself swept up into someone's stream of consciousness – or be whisked away into a fresh story of your own. It's unpredictable and not for the fainthearted. Look, I think we're almost there, wherever we're meant to be. The Invisible Woman would still be here otherwise. There seems to be a clearing up ahead. That must be where she wants us to go."

The path they'd been following had twisted and turned like a plot in a novel and Freddie hoped they could stop soon and take stock of where they were and what they were supposed to be doing. He liked to know what was what and he was a little nervous when he thought about how far he was from home. No one could ever find him here, was the thought that kept repeating in his head. If anything really bad was to happen, they would never *ever* find him. And now their guide had disappeared too!

As if reading his thoughts once again, Meg turned to him. "Stop worrying, Freddie. Look, nothing bad is going to happen." She paused. "Probably." She laughed at the look on Freddie's face. "Come on."

The trees opened out into a clearing which flickered with light and life. Around the edges, lanterns hung from what looked like shepherds' crooks, swaying in the night air. Creatures Freddie couldn't quite see moved about in the boughs overhead and he felt the paper weight of their curious glances. Whispers floated down to them. The trunks here all seemed to have doors and intricate carvings and Freddie studied the one closest to him. There were finely etched patterns and whorls carved into the wood, as well as eyes and faces, limbs and flowers. Up close, it was a bit of a masterpiece and he found himself engrossed in studying it. The longer he looked, the more there was to see.

A rustle above his head made him glance upwards. His mouth gaped. "Meg!" he hissed. "There are *words* growing on this tree."

Meg joined him. "It *is* a Story Forest, Freddie. Completely natural, I assure you." She grinned. "I found a sign – literally."

"Huh?" Freddie followed Meg to a little wooden sign stuck into the ground at the far edge of the clearing. As he read it aloud it grew upwards to reveal more and more text:

'Pick the seeds for your story, then feed them to a page.

Add a sprinkle of adventure and marinate in magic.

You may seek a red herring, a tantalising twist or a cliff-hanger.

Make your choice wisely.

Pin down any other interesting ideas along the way.

Question: Are you hero or villain?

Let the story decide!

Good luck in the Story Forest.'

"What on earth's *that* supposed to mean?" said Freddie.

"It means, Freddie," said Meg, eyes flashing like kingfishers, "that the Story Forest wants us to play."

Chapter Nine

Storytellers

"So, how do we 'pick the seeds' for our story?" asked Freddie. It all sounded a bit bizarre to him but he was intrigued by this Story Forest and as long as no wolves, witches or other undesirables appeared, he was willing to give whatever it was they were supposed to be doing a go.

"We're going to create our own story, so …" Meg looked around them. "I suppose seeds grow on trees?"

"Well, normally, yes," said Freddie, giving the Book-Keeper a perplexed look. "Here, they seem to be growing letters, as I was saying earlier."

"Oh, of course!" Meg slapped her forehead. "Don't you see, Freddie? The seeds *are* the letters! The letters are the seeds of the stories. We pick our seeds and then we —"

"Feed them to a page, I know," said Freddie. "But what, exactly, does the Story Forest mean by 'feed'? Why not say 'write' or 'put'?"

"We'll just have to wait and find out," said Meg. "Best gather our story seeds first and then we'll see what happens."

Freddie couldn't really see what all this had to do with saving Portsteven Library but he decided it was best to do as Meg said and it did actually sound quite fun. He'd certainly never created a story by picking living letters from a tree before. He reached up to a low-hanging branch and plucked a few random words and individual letters. As soon as he did, the tree budded with the nubs of replacements.

"Al*right*," said Freddie. "Clever old tree." He could have sworn the tree rustled its branches in pleasure at the compliment.

The words and letters were green and waxy, like proper leaves. Freddie filled his pockets with some from a few different trees and met Meg in the middle of the clearing again when he was finished.

"Now for a page or two," said Meg. "Let's go hunting!"

***

Unlike words, pages didn't grow on trees in the Story Forest. Unseen creatures twittered and giggled as they walked deeper in amongst them, leaving the clearing behind. As they passed trunk after trunk, Freddie felt the urge more and more to knock on one of their doors. "Maybe someone lives inside who can help us," he said. Meg nodded to go ahead.

Freddie gave a confident 'rap, rap, rap' with his knuckles on the nearest door. He waited for a few seconds but it remained closed. There was no handle to try opening it himself. He knocked on the next one and the next, each time his knocking growing a little quieter as his confidence faded.

"Surely *one* of them has to open?" he wondered aloud.

He jumped as the door he had just walked away from swung inwards with a gentle creak. Darkness seeped out and with it, a flash of white. It rushed past Freddie and bumped into Meg, bouncing off her to land on the grass.

"What the heck?" said Freddie.

Meg beamed. "I think we've found our page!"

Freddie looked at her, baffled. A voice from the ground piped up. "Do you have words, storytellers?"

"We do," said Meg.

"Then, yes, you have found your page," said the page, dusting itself off and standing tall.

Freddie couldn't help but stare. It was a page alright, smooth, white and spotless and it stood almost as tall as them both. It had a rubbery head, with arms and legs that looked like pencils, or tiny stilts. It was eyeing up their bulging pockets.

Meg looked at Freddie. "Let's feed it and see what happens." She gave the page a handful of letters and it stuffed them greedily into its mouth.

"More!" it demanded.

Meg fed it the rest of her loot, followed by Freddie with his. He watched in disgust as the page crammed more and more words and letters into its mouth, crunching noisily and not always with its mouth closed. As it ate, the single page opened out into a double page spread. When it had finished, it gave a loud burp and then sighed.

"Gross," muttered Freddie.

"Do you want your story or not?" the page glared at him.

Freddie stared back, refusing to be intimidated by a blank page. "Yes, please. I've just never seen a page eat words before. And so quickly," he said sweetly.

"Hmm, well, *manners*. I'll let it pass this time."

Freddie thought that was a bit rich after what he'd just witnessed, but he said nothing. Besides, he was much more interested in what was happening with the page's body. The white was slowly starting to fill with a jumble of letters and words; the ones the page had just eaten.

"Ah, stories taste so much better when they come from someone else," sighed the page. "Now, let's see what *yours* is about. I hope you chose sensibly."

Freddie had picked his words and letters completely at random, so he was just as curious as the page. His stomach did a quick somersault as he waited for the mass of letters to form coherent sentences. He just hoped they'd written a good story. He peered at the page, which promptly turned its back on him and shuffled away.

"Spoilers!" the little creature said huffily.

"But we have to *read* it, surely?" said Freddie.

The page's laugh sounded like someone scrunching up paper. "Don't be ridiculous! That would spoil the suspense. You give me the raw materials to reveal the story structure and the forest does the rest."

"But how —"

The page sighed. It was what it seemed to like doing best, other than eating words, Freddie thought. "I'm a page. I'm part of the fabric of the forest, just one of many living, connected parts. Now, the story has been written. Off you go! I've added in your sprinkle of adventure and the magic, well, that will come … Whether you fall for a red herring or a cliff-hanger remains to be seen. You can pick up other elements along the way."

"So, we can still choose things to shape the story?" asked Freddie. "I'm confused. I thought you just said our story was already written?"

"The Story Forest is different for everyone, Freddie," said Meg. "Perhaps our instructions aren't what someone else would get. Anyway, the beauty of any story is that it isn't set in stone."

The page looked as if it was about to disagree with

that but then pursed its lips together.

"*We* decide what happens – how it ends," said Meg. "The story structure is all we've created here on the page and even that's flexible. We can edit as we go."

The page looked a bit put out at that but again, stayed silent.

"Let's go, then?" said Freddie.

Meg nodded.

They both jumped as a door slammed behind them. The page had gone.

"Back into his tree," muttered Freddie.

"Quickest way for the story to be absorbed into the system, I'll bet!" said Meg. "Now, let's go and see what adventures we can have before we take you home!"

Chapter Ten

Catching Ideas

They followed fairy paths on into the heart of the forest, fireflies mixing with moonlight so it looked as if everything was dusted with gold and silver. Freddie knew they were now most definitely on fairy paths as he kept seeing tiny silhouettes out of the corner of his eye – shimmering, colourful shapes of otherworldly bodies which melted into the tree-scape when Freddie tried to look directly at them. He heard the musical whirring of wings and the glassy tinkle of laughter as they skipped out of reach.

A screech rent the air from somewhere in the Story Forest and Freddie hoped it was just an owl. He didn't want *that* sort of adventure. Up ahead, he spotted black and white shapes snuffling about on the ground.

"Badgers," said Meg. "Let's go and talk to them."

"Talk … to, er, badgers?"

Meg grinned. "Here, we still communicate with our creatures," she said. "Especially in the Story Forest. They're used to storytellers and adventurers passing through."

Freddie wondered what would happen if he tried talking to a badger back home. Somehow, he didn't think it would go very well. He tried to make himself look as non-threatening as possible as he approached this particular pair. He was still expecting them to bolt, despite what Meg had said.

"Let me guess, more storytellers and would-be adventurers," grumbled one of the badgers in a thick, gravelly voice.

"Now, Bay, we haven't actually met many adventurers recently. Be nice," chided the other badger in a similarly rasping voice. "How can we help you two, then?"

"I'm not sure," said Meg. "We're just passing through. I was showing Freddie the forest and it invited us to play but we don't have very much time, so we're just seeing what's what."

"Oh, so you aren't even proper adventurers, then!"

exclaimed Bay. "Typical."

"A minute ago you didn't want to meet *any* adventurers," said the second badger, sighing. "So hush now and let me handle this."

Bay grunted and shuffled off, rooting around in the undergrowth.

"Sorry about that. Well, I don't really know how I can help you. If I were you, I'd just keep going – it's the best way with the forest. It will reveal what it wants and you can make of it what you will!"

"Er, thanks. I think," said Freddie.

"No problem!" said the badger cheerfully. "In fact, look over there." Freddie looked to where its snout was pointing and thought he saw something shimmering. "Ideas are in the air tonight," said the badger. "Perhaps you might like to catch one?"

Freddie turned back to ask how and what, really, was the badger on about, but his informant had ambled off to join Bay and the two of them moved deeper into the forest, away from him and Meg. Where the animal had been, however, there now lay a butterfly net. Or, rather, thought Freddie dubiously, a net for catching *ideas*?

"Worth a try," he muttered, picking it up.

Meg nodded her approval. "Always useful, badgers," she said. "Even when you think they aren't. Let's see what we can catch then, Freddie. Tread carefully. We don't want to frighten them away."

Freddie tip-toed towards the floating ideas, which seemed to bob on the air like bubbles. The shimmering, as it turned out, was actually created by the effect of a few bauble-shaped ideas clustered together. They looked like they were dancing. It was the only word that sprang to mind when Freddie saw them up close. Each idea swirled with colour and was quite mesmerising. Indeed, Freddie almost forgot what he was there to do, but he remembered just in time and swished the net up and over the little group. Giggles exploded around him and Freddie saw colours flashing away into the forest. In his net, however, fluttered an idea.

"Great job," said Meg behind him. "They like a bit of hide and seek, ideas, but there's always one to be caught! What did you get?"

"I don't know. How do we find out?"

"Simple. We eat it."

Freddie looked at Meg, aghast. Then he looked at the idea and back again to the Book-Keeper. "You're joking, right? I mean, it looks *alive*."

"All ideas are alive, Freddie. But to make them grow and realise their ambitions they have to be consumed. Don't worry, they're not alive in the sense that *we* are. They won't feel anything. It's hard to explain, so you'll just have to trust me, OK? Come on, we'll split it."

Freddie didn't look convinced. "You first," he muttered, shoving the net towards Meg. She grinned, then reached into the net and grasped the idea. Freddie watched as she bit it roughly in half. More giggling filled the air as she did and golden sparks fizzled away from the seam of what was left. The Book-Keeper popped her half into her mouth, chewed, then swallowed. She shivered. "Delicious. And *interesting*. Go on, your turn."

Freddie reached for his part of the idea with a quivering hand. He couldn't believe he was doing this. Slowly, he lifted it to his mouth. It felt cool and squishy in his hand and it laughed as he stuffed it inside and chewed.

It was like eating a mixture of candyfloss and popping candy; marshmallows and ice cream. It was like living cloud, flavoured with rainbows. Freddie knew that he didn't actually know what rainbows tasted of but he was pretty sure it was like this idea. When he swallowed, the idea slid down his oesophagus and into his stomach like a refreshing dream. "Wow," he said.

"Exactly. Good ideas are rather marvellous, aren't they?" said Meg.

"And delicious and moreish," said Freddie with a grin. "Let's get some more."

Just at that moment the forest creaked. It was as if all of the trees had collectively stretched their ancient limbs. Pinpricks of light speckled the air and a wind rushed past them.

"What was that?" asked Freddie.

"I think that was a plot twist," whispered Meg. "Tends to happen with good ideas; they lead you in new directions."

A glittering path had appeared a little way ahead of them and Freddie stepped towards it. "Looks like we're going this way," he said.

The path twisted through the trees like a golden ribbon, winking in the moonlight. It led them into even denser forest and at last, to a glade full of fairies.

Chapter Eleven

Fey

Freddie thought that finding fairies was a fine sort of a plot twist. Wait till Brain and Rob heard about *this*. Well, wait until they heard about *everything* from tonight.

The fairies floated like wishes in the night sky, always just beyond reach. The effect was almost hypnotic as Freddie watched them weaving in and around each other in the air, laughing and singing. Magic pulsed from them in waves; Freddie felt the warm fuzzy glow of it as he stood, mesmerised.

"Don't stare, Freddie," said Meg. "That's how they lull you into a stupor. You don't know where you might end up if they do!"

"Right, of course," said Freddie, shaking himself

back to reality. Well, the reality of this strange night. A nearby fairy glared at Meg and she smirked back. It threw something which hit the Book-Keeper on the nose, then darted away, chuckling.

"Oi!" said Meg, rubbing her nose.

Freddie picked up the offending object, which he saw to his delight was a tiny gold flute. "What'll I do with this?" he asked. "Can I keep it?" His eyes shone with hope.

"No, nope, not in a million years," said Meg, shaking her head. "It's another fairy trick. If you steal or *take* something from a fairy that wasn't freely given then they'll exact their revenge and let me tell you, it just isn't worth the hassle."

"But he – or she – threw it at you. Surely that means it was freely given? It'd be brilliant to bring this back to show my friends, Brain and Rob."

"I wouldn't ..." warned Meg, raising an eyebrow.

Freddie noticed the fairy watching him a little way off and sighed. Perhaps it wasn't worth the risk. He put the flute on a tree stump and left it at that. No fairy loot for him. He was just about to ask Meg 'what now' when the fairy music and dancing stopped. It was as if someone had just snuffed out a candle. One minute the glade was giddy with fairy-light and frolicking, the next it was dark, empty and silent as a graveyard.

"Erm, where did they all go?" asked Freddie.

Meg shushed him with a finger to her lips. "When fey just disappear like that it means something's up," she whispered. "And it's never anything good. Come on, I think it's best if we go too."

A loud crunching sound came from behind them and Meg paled in the moonlight. "Oh no," she whispered.

"What? Hey, look," Freddie pointed to several mounds which had appeared in the glade, almost like molehills. More talking animals?

Suddenly, one of them erupted and something grey and greasy emerged from the earth. As they watched, more and more eruptions happened simultaneously, with similarly grotesque creatures slithering out from each one. They were long and muscular, their skin oozing what looked like some sort of slimy substance. Freddie couldn't see any eyes but the beasts collectively swivelled their heads towards him and Meg, and when one yawned, he caught a glimpse of razor-sharp teeth. Frozen, he stared at the assembled bodies.

And then they moved.

"Run – now!" shouted Meg.

On reflex, Freddie snatched up the abandoned fairy flute, then charged after Meg. They rushed noisily through the Story Forest as the things gave chase. Freddie wasn't sure he was being the hero of this tale but he reckoned he'd rather be in one piece to attempt that another day. Meg knew what she was talking about and if she said 'run', he trusted that she was right.

He heard slithering sounds behind them and willed his legs to pump harder. Where on earth was the exit? He had no idea which way they'd come; he just hoped Meg did. They fled past countless unrecognisable trees and over a bridge Freddie knew they definitely hadn't crossed before, but the trees gradually thinned and at last, they broke out of the Story Forest and were running back towards a shimmering bubble-like window suspended in the air, which he hoped was the mirror.

It was.

They jumped through it and Meg watched anxiously for excruciating seconds, then breathed a deep sigh of relief.

"Just checking they couldn't follow us back

through," she said in response to Freddie's questioning eyes.

"What *were* they?"

"Book Worms. Adolescents by the looks of things but still, dangerous."

Freddie knew he was staring but he was at a loss as to how he should react to that.

"Er, *book*worms? You mean, like—"

"Huge worms which eat books and therefore libraries. Oh, and Book-Keepers too. Think that about sums it up," said Meg.

"Ah …" said Freddie. "Scarier than my version of them, then."

They both laughed nervously.

"Also …" Meg's gaze slid away from Freddie and she fidgeted with her cuff.

"There's more?"

"Uh huh. A bit more."

"I take it that it isn't good." Freddie groaned. "OK, go on – out with it."

"Well, the Book Worms are dangerous enough on their own but unfortunately, they're *not* on their own anymore. A few years ago they joined leagues with, or came under the control of – no one's quite sure which way round it is – a rebel Book-Keeper called Hallow."

"What do you mean, a *rebel* Book-Keeper?"

"There haven't been many in our history but occasionally Book-Keepers are born who just don't love books and stories the way they ought to." Meg shrugged. "It's an anomaly. We're not like humans in that way, as *you* can have people who never read at all and no harm is done – other than they live a life unenriched by words … But Book-Keepers are a race born out of books – we exist solely to safeguard stories of all kinds. It's in our genetic makeup. So, when a Book-Keeper is born who *doesn't* have that vocation, they tend to become outcasts."

"That's hardly fair, if they're born that way," said Freddie.

"It's not that we shun them," said Meg hurriedly. "How can I explain? Our whole world – our lives – are centred around stories and a Book-Keeper born without that essence we all have seems to be repelled by our *world*, somehow, not by us as Book-Keepers. No matter how inclusive we try to be, they just seem to eventually drift away and leave our community. It's sad, really. No one knows where they go but there are all sorts of realms beyond this one where they might end up – alternative realities to ours. However, sometimes these lone Book-Keepers develop a hatred of everything to do with Book-Keepers, books and stories – and that's when there's trouble."

"Is that what happened with Hallow?"

"Yes. He didn't just drift away. He chose to stay and ever since he became an adult he's been trying to sabotage our work. His hatred has festered for years and now he's allied with the Book Worms, making both him and them twice as dangerous. Some think his hatred is so intense because he was born to two like him. In most cases, one parent – or both – are as most Book-Keepers are, but it's said that *both* Hallow's parents came from outside the Book-Keeper community. They abandoned him as soon as he could fend for himself and no one knows what became of them."

"That's awful," said Freddie. "And where does Hallow live now?"

"He's here, somewhere in our world, we *think*. But we're not sure whether he lives alone, with Book Worms, or whether he actually hides out in an entirely different reality and simply travels here when he wants to wreak havoc. Either way, he's not someone you'd want to run into. Hopefully we won't, but he's always trying to find ways to get rid of stories, so he's bound to have heard about our attempts to save Portsteven Library and wants to stop us."

"Huh, sounds like he has more than a little in common with Mr Tipett, the LAB inspector who's trying to close down Portsteven Library," said Freddie. "And one of *him* is bad enough." He shuddered. "Can we go now? We can talk more in my house if you like, but I've been gone a while and if my parents wake up ..."

"OK," said Meg. "You've probably seen enough for now, anyway. Enough to know that we Book-Keepers exist, that stories are living, breathing, marvellous things and that there are all sorts of adventures to be found in books."

"And out of them," said Freddie with a wry smile. "Also, Book Worms aren't just people with their noses stuck in a book all day and they're in league with a devious, dangerous Book-Keeper called Hallow."

"Yes, and that. Come on. Back to the Travelling Tree."

***

Like most return journeys, the way back to Freddie's house seemed to take less time than it had taken to get to the Book-Keepers' town. When he stepped out of the bookcase and back into the study it was with a quiet sigh of relief that he'd got home safely. He didn't want to imagine how his parents would feel if they'd woken in the morning to find him gone.

Meg blew more coloured dust into his eyes and muttered her spell and before he knew it, Freddie found himself rushing upwards and back to his normal size. He felt a little wobbly and disoriented when he was himself again, as if he'd stood up too quickly, so he sat down on the floor. Meg climbed the bookcase and sat dangling her legs over one of the shelves.

"So, I have another question," said Freddie. "Why me? Why am I the one you've chosen to help save the library?"

"Why not you?"

"Well … First of all, I don't really read books," mumbled Freddie, his face warming. He was glad it was still dark and the moon threw only a little light into the room. "So, I'm not sure I'm the best person to help save a library. I couldn't even manage to create a proper story in the Story Forest and it's full of everything you need to do that!"

Meg had been staring off into space as he spoke. She turned now to Freddie, eyes gleaming.

"We were very rudely interrupted by the Book Worms so don't worry about not completing your story. Anyway, I think I've figured out what the Invisible Woman was doing. The mirror shows different people different things, like I said before, and what it showed us – *you* – was a beautiful landscape coloured with the magic of storytelling *but* which was quickly polluted by those horrible Book Worms."

"I still don't think *I* get it."

"It's a metaphor made real!" Meg rolled her eyes at Freddie's quizzical look. "You'd be more familiar with them if you read more books," she reprimanded him. "The Invisible Woman was showing us the world with books and stories and also, the thing which can quickly destroy them – turning the fun, adventure and magic into mayhem and destruction. I think it was her way of telling us to hurry up and save the library, basically, and to show you a hint of just how wonderful and *necessary* stories are. They deserve to be saved, or the light of the world diminishes."

Freddie frowned. "If the library closes down then my mum's also out of a job and lots of people won't be able to use it for all sorts of things."

"Yes, but don't you see? It's about all of that, of course, but also, so much *more*," said Meg. "Stories and books can take anyone anywhere in the world – and far beyond it. You don't need to be a Book-Keeper to travel to space or to the other side of the world, or, or, to Fairyland, or wherever. That's the power – the magic – that books have. And libraries make all of that available to everyone for free. They also keep us Book-Keepers connected to your world, so we can keep taking care of the books and help people find the stories that are best suited to them.

"If the library closes down – if *any* library closes down – we lose all of that and there's a lot less magic in the world; we starve our imaginations and part of what makes us tick. Without books, people lose perspective; they grow selfish and less caring. I've seen it. Reading a book is like walking in someone else's skin for a while. You learn to see things from other people's points of view and you become more tolerant and understanding. And what's more, you do all of that – *become* all of that – without even knowing it, while you're having fun reading a book!"

Meg paused for breath.

"My mum and dad used to read me books at bedtime," said Freddie. "I do like books about space but maybe I should give fiction another go ..."

"I'll help you find something brilliant to read," said Meg, eyes shining. "Something to help you fall in love with books. Anyway, back to your question of 'why you'. I say again, why *not* you? Why anyone? Practically, I guess it's partly because your mum is the head librarian and you care about the library staying open, whether you're an avid reader or not. We're not allowed to appear to adults – too many problems from that – but kids are fine, so I figured you were the perfect choice."

"You don't know my mum," said Freddie, smiling. "She'd probably be OK with seeing you."

"Maybe, but best not to risk it. She's got enough on

her plate anyway. Secondly, part of our job as Book-Keepers is to match readers to books they'll really love and I guess part of that also means encouraging non-readers to pick up a book. So … you're ideal!

"OK, I'm convinced," said Freddie, laughing. "But how are we going to save Portsteven Library?"

And so, Freddie and Meg talked until the moon began to wan and dawn broke, conjuring up ideas about how to help the library. Yawning, Freddie said goodbye at last and crept back to bed, his head full of everything he'd seen and discussed that night.

Morning came much too soon, of course, but eating his porridge, a bleary-eyed Freddie felt excitement bubble in his veins. The library might be in danger but surely with the Book-Keepers on his side – and all of that story magic – they could put up a good fight for survival.

Chapter Twelve

Bookish Committees & Silver Surfers

The truth was, Meg didn't really know 'why Freddie' herself, if she really thought about it. It was rare that the Book-Keepers made contact with humans but they'd learned from past mistakes about trying to do everything themselves. Sometimes, you just needed a bit of outside help and, with the growing Book Worm problem, the Book-Keeper community of Thesaurus had voted in favour of involving Freddie. Well, a child. A conscientious, book-loving child to be precise, so Meg hadn't told them yet that she'd selected a boy who didn't read books and who, more to the point, didn't seem to particularly even *like* them.

"A minor issue," she muttered to herself the next

day, as she got ready to debrief the rest of the Book-Keepers. "Anyway, Freddie already seems more interested in stories. I'll help convert him into a reader and that'll be even better …"

In the meantime, however, she had to report back on their first meeting. The Book-Keepers were depending on Meg to do her bit and she didn't want to disappoint them. She sighed as she gathered her things together. The Book-Keepers were a notoriously secretive race who liked to keep themselves to themselves, which was why they hadn't asked to meet Freddie in person. They trusted her to have chosen someone suitable for the task at hand; it was always left to the younger Book-Keepers to make contact with human children when such contact was needed, as only children were allowed in those rare circumstances to see them. Never adults. It was just the way it had always been. As to why Meg was the Book-Keeper chosen for the task, well, *that* was an entirely different matter altogether and not one she liked to think about if she could help it.

She swung a bag onto her shoulder and called goodbye to her mum, closing the cottage door gently behind her. Most Book-Keepers didn't like a lot of noise

– perhaps it came from spending so much time in quiet libraries and other bookish places. She hurried down the path which split their garden – a colourful confusion of wildflowers, herbs and vegetables – and let herself out through the little blue gate at its end. They lived at the north of Thesaurus, tucked around a corner away from their nearest neighbours and it was a ten-minute brisk walk into town. Meg was to meet with the group of Book-Keepers currently elected to manage the general running of Thesaurus. New Book-Keepers were chosen every year, so everyone had their turn in taking responsibility for the efficient running of their home. Meg therefore knew them all very well, but she was still a little nervous about giving her report on Freddie.

She'd arranged to meet the committee at the town hall, a large building made of dictionaries – one large tome for the roof and lots of smaller dictionaries as bricks. With all their adventures last night, Meg hadn't had time to fill Freddie in on quite a few things about her home, not least that the books they used for building were enchanted to protect them from the elements. It was a novice Book-Keeper indeed who tried to construct a house from ordinary books, as all their hard work quickly turned into a soggy mess when it rained. Book-Keeper children soon found that out for themselves when they played at 'keeping house' with non-enchanted tomes, for of course, the enchanted versions were too precious to waste on games.

The town hall was lofty inside, with a high ceiling and various smaller rooms leading off from the main space. Meg made her way to one of these inner chambers, where she found the committee waiting for her. She was on time but still felt as if she'd turned up late. All eyes turned to her as she entered. She scanned the faces around the circular table – Mayor Winifred Thorne, a book-binder by trade, gave her a welcoming smile. Beside her sat Deputy Mayor Sonya Bell, the town's choir mistress, then there was Ms Rosemary the baker, Mr Peppen the repair man, Mr Sawyer the builder and Mrs Nestler, who helped look after the Travelling Tree. Beside her sat an alchemist called Mrs Barbery, then came Mr Threadley the tailor, Mr Copperware the chef, artist Ms Mulberry and finally, Mr Zachary – or rather, *Professor* Zachary.

The Book-Keepers' primary task was always to look after books, of course, but they also had to live their own daily lives, as all creatures do, so most of the community had a separate profession. Meg was in training to be an alchemist.

"Thank you for coming, Meg," said Mayor Thorne. "I'm sure you had an eventful evening yesterday but if you can just fill us all in on how things went, then we'll let you get back to your duties."

Meg cleared her throat. "Well, I managed to speak with a boy – Freddie – he's the son of the head librarian at Portsteven Library so I thought he'd be a good choice."

The councillors nodded in approval. Meg skipped over the part about Freddie not exactly being a big book lover (yet) and continued, "We went straight to the Hall of Eclectics as you said and …"

Everyone leaned forward in anticipation.

"She came," whispered Meg.

"The Invisible Woman?" asked Professor Zachary, excitement rippling across his face.

"Yes."

"What form did she take?" This came from Mrs Nestler.

"She was an orb of light," said Meg. "And she led us

through a mirror to the Story Forest."

The committee listened attentively as Meg told them the rest of what had happened, interrupting her a few times with questions. They seemed satisfied, however, with what she'd said and the meeting concluded swiftly after all was recounted. Meg agreed to keep everyone updated on how things progressed with Freddie and the humans, while they focused their energies on addressing the ever-growing Book Worm problem.

"We're worried that Hallow is going to make an appearance soon," said Mayor Thorne. She studied Meg carefully. "You *will* tell us at once if you come across him … or if he tries to make contact with you? It's unlikely, of course, but as you're the chosen Book-Keeper to act as go-between with the humans, he may well target you. And, er, of course." She paused. "There's the other matter of—"

"I'll let you know," said Meg quickly. "But I'll be very careful. I don't exactly *want* to meet him. I never have," she added.

"Of course you don't want to meet him!" said Mr Sawyer, his face reddening. "We only want you to be on extra alert – just in case. He's unpredictable and will no doubt see the potential demise of another library as the perfect opportunity for interference."

Meg nodded. There was nothing else to tell them, so she left the committee to discuss further defensive measures for Thesaurus and made her way to the building where she and her fellow alchemists trained. There was work to be done before her next meeting with Freddie.

***

Friday was everyone's favourite day at school as it heralded the beginning of the weekend and today, Freddie was even more restless than usual as he waited for the final bell to ring. He'd held back from telling Brain and Rob everything from the night before as he thought it might be more believable if they saw Meg for themselves first. Even he found it hard to believe that he'd travelled through a bookcase, a magic mirror and a Story Forest – and he was the one it had happened to.

Freddie and his friends rushed to the library after school.

"This'd better be good, Fred," said Rob, shaking his

head. "Spending Friday afternoon in the library!"

Of course, they had to wait a while until there were fewer people about, but it was quiet in Freddie's corner and he wanted Brain and Rob to have time to speak with Meg before the library closed, so he tapped the bottom of the bookcase, which they were all sitting around, pretending to do homework on their laps. Brain and Rob looked a little bored and Freddie drank in the looks on their faces with glee as the outline of Meg's door scratched itself into the wood and it swung slowly inwards. Meg's head popped around it and she grinned up at them. Rob's mouth dropped open, while Brain just stared from Meg to Freddie and back again.

They were all paying so much attention to Meg that no one noticed they had company until it was too late. Freddie jumped as a hand gripped his shoulder.

"Now then," said a voice. "What do we have here?"

***

Freddie kicked himself at having been so stupid. Why hadn't one of them kept watch? He'd been too carried away with trying to impress Brain and Rob. Now what?

He turned around and looked into the milky eyes of one of his mum's Silver Surfers. She wore thick purple glasses and lots of layers of clothing. She was leaning on a walking stick and her mouth formed a pale pink 'Oh' as she saw Meg pull the bookcase door closed with a click.

"My goodness," she breathed. "A Book-Keeper." Her eyes grew misty. "I haven't seen one of those in years, my dears. Well, boys, you'd better fill me in!"

Freddie swallowed. What did she mean, she hadn't seen one in years? Surely this pensioner hadn't seen a *Book-Keeper*? And if she had, why didn't anyone know about it? Then again, she'd just seen Meg and seemed to know exactly what she was, so she couldn't be lying. She certainly wasn't shocked. The old woman stuck out her hand. It was pale and soft as a silk pillow when Freddie clasped it in a handshake. Blue veins patterned the skin like ribbons.

"I'm Gwendoline Glass. Gwen for short." The old lady gave them a broad smile. "Oh, and that's Graham, my friend," she added, waving over at an elderly man with silver hair and a bushy beard who was dressed all in tweed. He raised his own walking stick in acknowledgement but stayed where he was. Freddie wasn't quite sure what was going on but he decided they'd just better go with it for now.

"How do you know about Book-Keepers?" he whispered, as Gwen shook hands with Brain and Rob. This was one too many a surprise for his friends and they crouched, mute, as Freddie questioned their intruder.

"I was once your age too, you know," said Gwen with a knowing smile. "Creatures such as Book-Keepers only tend to reveal themselves to the young as they have fresh enquiring minds unpolluted by reality and the daily doldrums." She pursed her lips and the ghost of a smile played across her face. "Perhaps that's why I managed to see that one," she pointed her stick at the bookcase. "I'm now at the other end of the scale, you see. I'm young at heart, nearing the end instead of being at the start, if you get my drift." She winked at the boys. "The older you get, the more susceptible you become to seeing the unusual again. If you talk about it, people assume you're doolally, so I don't think the wee folk mind *very* much if we glimpse them again! Anyway, it would be better if we talked somewhere else ..." Gwen glanced around the library. "What say you that we rendezvous tomorrow morning for a little tête-à-tête? We can discuss everything then, say at 11 o'clock at The Painted Pot?"

Freddie just stared at her. "Erm —"

"Tomorrow's Saturday, boys. What is it? Do you have other plans?" Gwen blinked slowly behind her big purple glasses.

Freddie glanced at Brain and Rob, who both shrugged.

"OK, see you then – Gwen," said Freddie.

Gwen beamed. "Righto, boys! Looking forward to it." She turned to go, then whirled back around and flicked her arm up as if she was waving an invisible wand. "Oh, and I'll bring Graham. Toodle-oo!"

As Gwen shuffled back to the other Silver Surfers, Freddie turned on his friends. "Thanks for the backup, guys! What are we supposed to do now?"

"You could have said 'no'," muttered Rob, avoiding eye contact with Freddie.

"How?" demanded Freddie.

"This day is beyond weird," said Brain, shaking his head.

They all looked at each other and Freddie felt laughter bubbling up unexpectedly inside him, despite what had just happened. It had certainly been a weird week for *him*, so why not round it off with an invitation to tea with two Silver Surfers to talk about a race of tiny people who lived behind the bookcases?

Brain and Rob were laughing now too and they laughed even harder when people began shooting them disgruntled looks and hissing at them to be quiet. When Mercury came over to see what all the fuss was about Freddie decided they'd better split. He waved goodbye to his friends, having agreed to keep their meeting with Gwen and Graham and he settled back down at his table to wait until closing time.

What surprises was Saturday going to deliver, he wondered?

Chapter Thirteen

Seaside Rendezvous at The Painted Pot

Freddie's mum was delighted to hear that her son and his friends were meeting up with Gwen and Graham.

She beamed. "They're two of my favourite Silver Surfers; kindred spirits, Fred. It'll be nice for you to get to know them. You can learn all sorts of interesting things from the elderly, you know. Long lives mean plenty of tales to tell! Gwen's daughter, Penny, owns The Painted Pot. She'll make sure you're well looked after."

The Painted Pot was at the bottom of the promenade, at the opposite end of the town from the library. It overlooked the harbour of fishing boats and was so-called because its walls were covered in paintings, ranging from the amateur artwork of those who attended the painting classes in the upstairs studio, to those which cost more than a month's mortgage payment, as Freddie's mum often remarked when they visited. Freddie usually couldn't distinguish the amateurs' work from the professionals' until he clocked the price tags and he wondered what would happen if he switched the prices on a few. Would the buyers think twice, or not at all, before handing over hundreds of pounds or more for an unknown painter's work? He liked to imagine the delight on an amateur artist's face at being handed a large cheque. Someday maybe he'd risk it, but not today.

Gwen waved enthusiastically at him as soon as he entered the café. Freddie had spent the morning so far at the library with his mum. She'd already spoken on the phone with Penny, who said she'd keep an eye on them all. There had been no appearance from Meg, despite Freddie's hopes. He'd realised he had no proper way of contacting her besides tapping on bookcases – and how reliable was that, really? He was just banking on the Book-Keeper appearing again and hoped she wouldn't be too angry when she did. They shouldn't have let themselves be seen. On the other hand, Gwen seemed to know about the Book-Keepers already, so maybe this would actually work in their favour.

"Er, hi," he said awkwardly, as he arrived at the corner table Gwen had chosen.

"I'm afraid I didn't catch your name yesterday, dear," said Gwen, continuing on as Freddie opened his mouth to speak, "but Penny tells me it's Freddie."

He nodded. "Penelope is my daughter," said Gwen, giving the red-cheeked woman behind the counter a wave. "I hope you don't mind, but I've already placed an order for a pot of Darjeeling, some scones and a selection of tray bakes. Well now, take a seat, Freddie! I'm sure your friends will be here soon."

Just at that moment, Brain and Rob appeared at the door, followed soon after by Graham, dressed in another smart tweed suit. Yesterday's outfit had been forest green while today's was a deep blue, complemented by a turquoise cravat. Freddie wondered if Graham had tweed suits in every colour of the rainbow.

"Excellent," said Gwen as everyone arranged themselves around the table and Penny brought over their tray of tea things. Once they'd all been served, Gwen leaned forward and gave them a conspiratorial look. "Right, let's get down to business."

***

Meg was still fuming with herself for allowing the old woman to see her – and now it was affecting her potions. She'd have to be careful. If she let her emotions get the better of her and slip into her mixtures, as they had just done, then they wouldn't work properly. She felt crowded by secrets all of a sudden and she wasn't sure she could handle any more of them. At least Freddie was showing signs of liking books now, after his visit to the Story Forest, so she was confident that his not being a reader wouldn't be a problem for much longer. She'd been *seen*, though. By an adult. The shame of it made her want to lie low for a while, but she knew she'd have to speak with Freddie soon. The library still needed saving, after all.

She studied the ingredients she was mixing and frowned. The trouble with being an apprentice alchemist was that all of your potions had to be meticulously inspected and graded until you passed through the training. There must be no trace of what had just happened within her mixtures, otherwise she might be forbidden from seeing Freddie again – library crisis or no library crisis – and then where would they be?

Meg bit her lip and sighed. She would just have to start again and then she really must go and see Freddie. The Book Worms were getting stronger and trouble was brewing on the outskirts of Thesaurus.

***

Trouble was indeed bubbling and brewing on the periphery of Thesaurus and Hallow thought things were simmering away rather nicely.

The Book Worms were slow-witted, lumbering creatures, but they shared a common passion and purpose and they were proving themselves to be rather useful. Hallow had plans, you see, and extra bodies were required. This latest library crisis linked to Thesaurus had refocused him – there were Book-Keeper communities all over the place, but it was this particular one which kept hooking him back to its borders.

Libraries were closing down at an exponential rate these days in what humans called the 'United Kingdom', as well as elsewhere, so Hallow happily had lots of easy pickings when it came to eradicating Earth of books. Personal interest *did* make victory taste all the sweeter, however, so he just hadn't been able to resist returning to his birthplace. Of course, it was also significant because of that other, foolish experiment he'd once attempted, the product of which could be about to cause him a spot of trouble. Well, thorns could be pulled from sides and nuisances dealt with. He wasn't going to let anything spoil his fun.

And it *was* fun, destroying books. Hallow smirked. Everyone knew that the ignorant and the unimaginative were much more malleable – more easily manipulated and controlled. Cut off their supply of stories and creative genius, and the possibilities for destruction were endless.

Hallow had spent his whole life an outcast, without vocation or empathy for anyone but himself. He loathed the Book-Keeper community which had birthed him into abandonment, creating an anomaly who couldn't fit in because, apparently, his DNA was all wrong. His genetic makeup had carried him away from the life he should have had – one which he just couldn't see the appeal of, no matter how hard he tried. And he *had* tried, at first, but his brain was just wired differently.

He didn't belong.

Surely someone had to pay for that?

He'd been developing something for a while now, on the side of his library activities, and it was just about time, he thought, to put his plan into action.

***

By the end of his visit to The Painted Pot, Freddie had learned that Gwen wrote historical romance novels and Graham was a former university physics professor. Perhaps that was why Gwen's fellow Silver Surfer took the news of the Book-Keepers so calmly, Freddie thought. His probing, scientific mind was open to any possibility and he seemed content, for now, to accept as evidence everyone else's word at having seen a Book-Keeper as proof that they existed.

Graham was more of a listener than a contributor and Gwen talked enough for all of them. She'd met her tweed-loving friend when they both joined the Silver Surfers Club at the library to "brush up on our tech skills," as she put it. As for her Book-Keeper sighting of old, Gwen explained that she'd made friends with a Book-Keeper boy she discovered in the mobile library van that used to go through her village when she was a girl. She had never visited the Book-Keepers' world and was very excited to hear all about Freddie's adventure in the Story Forest and Thesaurus. She had, however, enjoyed frequent conversations with Robin, as he had been called, when she visited the van every week ("I was – and remain – a bit of a bookworm!"), until he just didn't appear one day – and never did again.

"I was worried at first that something had happened to him, but I was an avid reader, you see, so I knew in my heart what had really happened," said Gwen sadly. She rolled her eyes at the boys' blank expressions. "I grew up! I probably saw Robin for longer than I should have because I was so open to the idea of him, but we all grow up in the end and there are rules which must be kept to." She paused for a sip of tea. "They're a bit like Borrowers, aren't they? Only I suppose they don't really borrow our things ..."

As they polished off the scones and tray bakes, more than a few things were shared and decided, to the effect that by the time they were packing up to leave, ("Don't worry dears – this is on me and Penny today!") they had formed a very unusual book club comprising two Silver Surfers and three boys who really didn't read very much ("Speak for yourself," said Brain when Rob mentioned it). It would act as the perfect cover for their meetings to discuss plans to save the library.

Freddie had agreed to try and make contact again with Meg, to see how her plans were shaping up, while Gwen said she and Graham would investigate Mr Tipett and "poke around a bit."

"We'll put our internet search skills to the test!" she said, waving her walking stick and almost hitting Rob in the face.

They would also ask about the peaceful protest Freddie's mum had mentioned. All in all, things had got done, other things had been earmarked for doing and Freddie, Brain and Rob found they had made two new, if rather unexpected, friends.

Chapter Fourteen

One Vision

Freddie spent the rest of the weekend trying to summon Meg. On the way home on Saturday – his mum finishing up early at work – they'd stopped at a second-hand shop and bought a small pre-loved bookcase for Freddie's bedroom. Mercury was delighted at her son's newfound interest in literature, which made him feel a little guilty. The real reason he wanted a bookcase, of course, was so that he could more easily contact Meg, without having to creep around the house at night. However, Freddie realised that all this talk of books and Book-Keepers and stories (Gwen having also regaled them with tales of her own writing) had genuinely sparked his interest.

So many people, including his own parents, were in

love with words and the magic they seemed to weave and he'd decided he wanted to re-engage with books and see if he could enjoy them as much as everyone else did. So, he added a couple of second-hand paperbacks filled with adventure stories to his bookcase purchase, while his mum tried and failed to smother a beatific smile.

The problem was, it hadn't worked.

It was now Sunday night and no amount of tapping on wood or whispering at the bookcase had resulted in a visit from Meg. The books, on the other hand, were proving to be very interesting, but Freddie was starting to worry that he'd never see Meg again. The Painted Pot Book Club, as they'd named themselves, was due to meet again on Friday afternoon. What would Freddie do, he wondered, if he wasn't able to get hold of his Book-Keeper friend before then?

As it turned out, his fears were rootless after all, for as the clock struck midnight on Sunday, Freddie was awoken by the sound of tiny knuckles on wood. Only half-awake, he squinted in the dark and felt for the lamp switch at the side of his bed. Blinking in the buttery light, Freddie scanned the room, his gaze snagging on his new bookcase.

"Meg, is that you?" he whispered.

"Affirmative. Why, who else were you expecting?"

Meg climbed onto the second shelf of the bookcase and sat, dangling her legs over the edge. Freddie left his warm bed to join her, shivering as the chill of the room beyond his snuggly duvet wrapped itself around his body.

"Ha, ha. No one, of course," he said. "It's just that I've been looking for you since the day we were interrupted in the library …"

"Yeah, sorry about that. The old lady startled me. I'm not usually so clumsy with the camouflage, but I heard what she said to you and it checks out. She met a Book-Keeper called Robin when she was a child. It's good to hear that she kept it a secret all this time, although, there's not many who would believe her if she told anyone, anyway.

"As for why the wait to chat, well, I was busy with a few things and it took me a while to find the way to your new bookcase." She rapped the wood. "It's had a long life and many have travelled through it but there are ways and means – *secret* ways and means," she added, as Freddie opened his mouth, "of tracking people down. Just takes a bit of time. We've also been having more Book Worm trouble, but nothing for you to worry about too much – yet. Anyway, here I am. What's been happening since we last spoke?"

Freddie felt the itch of a yawn. He was keen to dive back under his warm duvet, so he quickly filled Meg in on the Saturday meeting.

Meg nodded throughout the telling. "A protest sounds good," she said. "But we need to make a *lot* of noise, Freddie – get so many people involved that these LAB people have no choice but to listen and keep the library open. We need—"

"Publicity!" said Freddie, a thought flitting into his head and soaring swiftly, like a kite in the wind. "We need publicity and I know just how to get it. My dad's a newspaper editor in the city. If he runs a story then loads of people are bound to see it and help us. He could interview me and mum – and the Silver Surfers – and other people who use the library."

"That's a brilliant idea," said Meg. "I'm afraid that I'm not much help to you on this side of the bookcase, but I think you and your friends will make lots of the right noise for the library. What I *can* do, along with the other Book-Keepers, is help keep Hallow and the Book Worms at bay. They have an unnaturally grotesque talent of sniffing out decaying libraries and I'm afraid that your library is still very much on their radar. We've been experiencing more attacks than normal and everyone's working overtime at the minute to track them and try to keep them away."

"What, er, damage do they do, exactly?" asked Freddie.

"Well, to begin with, minor stuff, like nibbling at the pages of books and burrowing into bookcases. When a library's decaying – not being used very much, or at risk of closing down – that only speeds up the process of decay. *Then* they lay eggs inside the bookcases and the growing Book Worms feed on the wood and the books, consuming everything, basically, from the inside-out until there's nothing left. If a Book-Keeper gets in the way then they're toast, too. Book Worms are blind, like most worms, so they just tend to eat whatever's in their path. And I suppose we Book-Keepers *do* smell all bookish and woody …"

Freddie shivered as he recalled the sharp teeth of the

Book Worms from their Story Forest adventure.

"Anyway, they do a lot of damage and are more difficult to stop once an army takes root in a library," said Meg. "We're not quite at that stage with Portsteven Library yet, but that's why we need to act fast. We don't just have Book Worms seeking it out to lay eggs in, we also have full-grown worms which just want to go straight to devour mode."

"Yeah, we definitely don't want any of that," said Freddie. "I've just thought of another way to get publicity, too. I told my dad that I might get involved with the school radio this year and I've just decided who my first interviewee will be."

Meg raised her eyebrows. "Who?"

"Mr Tipett!"

Chapter Fifteen

Tipett Under Pressure

Freddie started putting the pieces of his plan together the very next day. He'd asked his mum at breakfast about getting in touch with Mr Tipett for the school radio interview.

"Oh, Fred, why on earth would you want to talk to that odious little man?" she said, before clamping her mouth shut and giving him an embarrassed smile. "I don't mean that. I'm sure he's a nice man at home, but I'm afraid he's not my favourite person at the minute, nor I his, I think. What on earth do you want with him?"

"I'm going to interrogate him about the library," said Freddie, between mouthfuls of milky porridge. "To help you," he added.

Mercury smiled. "That's a lovely gesture, Fred." She

sighed. "I'm not sure how much it'll help with Mr Tipett's decision-making, but you never know. I suppose it's worth a try. I'll write down his telephone number and you can give it to Ms Woods if the school agrees to invite him in."

"Thanks mum!"

Freddie knew Ms Woods would be delighted that he was showing an interest in the school radio, so he didn't expect any problems from that end. The only potential issue would be if Mr Tipett refused to come in for the interview. Somehow, though, Freddie suspected the LAB inspector would be only too eager to talk on the radio.

Well, Freddie would be ready for him.

***

Ms Woods was very interested indeed in Freddie's request to interview Mr Tipett, and Brain and Rob said they'd help out too.

"I'd heard that Portsteven Library was being inspected," she said, "and I think it would be awful for the town to lose it. Quite right, Freddie, to ask Mr Tipett to explain himself, when so many people use it and want it to stay open!"

"Are you going to come to the protest that's being planned, Ms Woods?" asked Freddie. "My mum's friend, Laurel, is organising one. I can let you know the details, if you like?"

Ms Woods puckered her lips and wiggled them from left to right, as if she was checking to see what a protest tasted like, then she relaxed them into a broad smile.

"Yes, Freddie, why not? It can't hurt, can it? I've always wanted to take part in a protest."

She asked Freddie, Brain and Rob to stay behind for a few minutes at the end of the day and Freddie hoped the triumphant look on her face was good news. It was.

"Boys! I spoke to Mr Tipett personally at lunchtime and I'm delighted to tell you that he has agreed to come into school tomorrow for the interview. I suggested Tuesday afternoon, as it's our usual class library time. It doesn't give you very long to get your questions ready, but I'm sure you can think of a fair few between now and then. Good luck!"

Freddie, Brain and Rob had already arranged to go to Portsteven Library after school, so they put their heads together as soon as they got settled at Freddie's usual table to think of suitably probing questions. Brain and Rob were disappointed that Meg wouldn't be visiting, but Freddie said they could come to his house another evening and see her in the safety of his bedroom. They seemed satisfied with that and got down to work.

Tuesday was going to be an important day and Freddie was determined to make his time with Tipett count.

***

By the time Tuesday afternoon arrived, Freddie had sweaty palms and his stomach felt as if someone was flipping pancakes inside it. As soon as he saw Mr Tipett's weedy frame at the door, the internal somersaulting stopped, however, and was replaced by something much more like fire in his belly. His questions, Freddie decided, would be like flames pouring from his mouth like an angry dragon …

"Freddie!"

Freddie jumped as he realised Mr Tipett was now standing right in front of him. Reading those adventure stories from the second-hand bookshop had obviously ignited his imagination. He smiled at that and Mr Tipett, thinking it was for him, gave a thin-lipped and completely insincere smile back. Freddie quickly dropped his own face into a neutral expression.

"Now, I've explained to Mr Tipett that the interview is broadcast live to the whole school but that we also record it for future reference and learning opportunities," said Ms Woods. "I'll leave you boys to it, then! I'll just be sitting quietly in the corner, so if you need me, wave."

It had been decided that Brain would introduce the interview, which would be led by Freddie, with Brain and Rob then chipping in if they felt the need. Rob was keeping an eye on the tech side of things and he held up his fingers to count Brain down to the intro.

And then, they were off.

After a brief welcome from Brain, Freddie kept his own opening comments short and sweet, asking Mr Tipett firstly to confirm his position as a local councillor and LAB board member. Both roles had, he thought, quite cloudy job descriptions attached to them, as Mr Tipett then went on to regale them with his general responsibilities. Despite his efforts to explain, however, it really wasn't very clear what else Mr Tipett did in the day when he wasn't going around upsetting Freddie's mother with library inspections.

Freddie's next question seemed to confuse Mr Tipett, who was quite happily rabbiting on about the equally non-descript department he worked for and probably would have kept talking about it all afternoon, had Freddie not interrupted. Politely, of course, as all good interviewers must.

"Mr Tipett," he said with a smile. "How would you describe yourself, for anyone who doesn't know you?"

"Describe myself?" Mr Tipett's eyebrows shot up, making him look like a startled rabbit.

"In, say, three words," said Freddie helpfully.

"Um, well … I suppose, possibly … kind, hard-working and, er, team-spirited," said Mr Tipett, somewhat triumphantly. He looked as if he'd just passed an important test and Freddie smiled to himself. This was nothing, yet.

"You sound like a very nice person," he said.

Mr Tipett nodded. "I am."

"And what do you like doing in your spare time?

What hobbies do you have?"

"Hobbies?" Mr Tipett frowned. "Well, I, ah, work very hard, you see … not much time for … Well, I suppose … fishing! Yes, fishing is a hobby I enjoy."

"Great," said Freddie. "I like *eating* fish – with chips."

"Lots of good chippies in the area," said Mr Tipett, nodding as if the success of the local takeaways was thanks to him, personally.

Freddie saw his opening. "Yes, our community has lots of great places to eat and to do other things," he said. "Do you care about our local community, then, Mr Tipett?"

"Why, of course, young Freddie!" Mr Tipett adjusted his glasses. "It's all part of my role as a local councillor and government employee – to care for and look after the community and its amenities. And, as a local resident too, of course," he added hurriedly, when Freddie raised his eyebrows at him.

"What about school and education? Do you think those are important too?"

"Why, yes, of course. They certainly are," said Mr Tipett, his eyes narrowing a little. "Education is vital! It means that you could get a job like mine one day, boys."

Freddie bit back a smile and he heard Brain and Rob smother snorts. No thanks, he thought. Not if it meant complete boredom and closing down people's public services.

"And to be educated, we need schools and easy access to learning and learning materials, don't we? You would agree that that's all important too? Especially if we can't afford to access these things otherwise?"

"Er, yes ..."

"Good." Freddie paused in what he hoped was suitably dramatic fashion. Mr Tipett was eyeing him nervously now, as if he was a fish wriggling on a hook about to be reeled in by the schoolboy opposite him.

"Libraries are perfect then, aren't they?" said Freddie. "They're free for the public to use and provide excellent learning resources for everyone, of every age."

"Ah, well, yes – but you see, young Freddie, they also cost money to run and —"

"Local governments have lots of money, though, don't they?" asked Freddie. "They get it so they can help their communities and it's up to them how they use that money for the wider good, isn't it?"

"Well, yes, but there's lots of things to spend it on

besides lib—"

"What do you think of Portsteven Library, Mr Tipett?" asked Freddie, adding pointedly, "Where my mum works?"

"I think I see where you're going with this, young Freddie, and I'm afraid I can't possibly comment on that," said Mr Tipett, now starting to visibly perspire. "All discussions concerning that library are confidential until I write and file my report."

"Oh, I don't mean pro*fess*ionally," said Freddie. "I mean, personally, what do you think of it? As a local resident?" He smiled sweetly as Mr Tipett scowled, seeing the trap he'd been led neatly into.

"Well, I think it's very good – quite good – of course," said Mr Tipett, "but it's old and a bit rough around the edges … needs work doing to it and that work costs money! And do we really know that it's used as much as some people say it is? I do wonder about that! We need to evaluate whether it, er, I mean …"

"Whether to close it?" Brain chipped in.

"Yeah," said Rob. "What are your plans for our town library? My granny uses it. *I* use it!"

"My sister and mum borrow books from it all the

time," said Brain. "And I do too. Plus, I sometimes do my homework there when my mum can't collect me after school."

"My mum works in it *and* our friends in the Silver Surfers use it for all sorts of things," added Freddie.

"What friends? What Silver Surfers?" asked Mr Tipett. "Never heard of them!"

"Is Portsteven in the running for 'Town of the Year' again this year?" asked Freddie, with what he hoped was an angelic expression on his face.

Mr Tipett looked thrown off-course by this sudden change of conversational direction.

"Yes – and we should win it too, by rights," he said, puffing out his chest like a limp balloon. "We were cheated the past two years. We're definitely the best town in the area."

"Hmm," Freddie frowned, as if he'd just realised something unfortunate. "If Portsteven was to lose an important educational and community hub like the town library, though, wouldn't that make our chances of winning 'Town of the Year' a bit, well, *tricky*, Mr Tipett? Wouldn't that make you, the town, the council *and* the Library Administration Body all look a bit bad?"

"Yeah – and uncaring," said Brain.

"And not very community-spirited," said Rob.

"Or *team*-spirited," added Freddie.

"Or … very *kind* at all," said Rob with a grin.

Mr Tipett, whose face was now tomato-red and covered in a fine sheen of sweat, spluttered and stood up rather shakily.

"Boys, I'm sorry, but I'm a *very* busy man and I must get back to the office. I'm afraid this interview is over!"

Chapter Sixteen

In Good Company

Mr Tipett stormed out of Portsteven Primary School, his upper lip tickling him with sweat and his nice clean shirt now rather soggy and smelling of body odour. How dare that boy – *Freddie* – with his bright ginger hair and mischievous eyes try to trick him like that? Lulling him into a false sense of security with all his silly talk of personal qualities and fish and chips. Bah. What had fish and *chips* got to do with anything, anyway? Was this what the prodigy of education looked like these days? Dim-witted questions from even more dim-witted boys? Although, perhaps he shouldn't have underestimated the librarian's son. There *he'd* been trying to demonstrate his kindness and community spirit by participating in a school radio interview, only to be ambushed the way he had. Maybe this boy Freddie was a bit cleverer than Mr Tipett had given him credit for.

The good news was that the school radio wasn't a proper station on the air, which might just be his saving grace thought Mr Tipett, as he reversed his Mini out of the school car park. Better the public never heard that excuse of an interview. It was a disgrace, that's what it was!

He swallowed. This wouldn't do at all. Now he was getting all stressed. Though the boy did have a point about the 'Town of the Year' award. He sniffed. Well, that just made it all the more important that he finish his report quickly and get rid of the library for good before judging time. They could make it into something *much* better, even if that meant simply knocking it down and planting a nice colourful flowerbed in its place. What use were books to anyone, anyway? Mr Tipett didn't know a single person who read the dratted things. Granted, he didn't really have any friends to check this with, but wasn't it all about computers and online things these days? Books took up desirable space, especially in seaside resorts like Portsteven, which needed more places to put up tourists when they came to stay …

No, Mr Tipett knew what was good for the town and he wasn't going to let a trio of annoying schoolboys put him off. He wouldn't be bullied into doing what they wanted, especially not without a good counter-argument. He just couldn't see the value of stories – he never had and he never would. He hadn't grown up with them, in fact, his father used to throw the few hardback books they had at home (boring, musty old business books) at his weedy son when he was angry with young Tipett. What had books ever done for *him*, eh? And look at him now – he'd turned out all right without them, hadn't he?

Mr Tipett's stomach growled. All this stress was making him hungry.

He decided to stop on the way back to the office for some fish and chips.

***

The boys all agreed the interview with Mr Tipettt had been a resounding success. He had certainly shown his true colours and, judging by the chatter amongst their class and the rest of the school afterwards, he wasn't anybody's favourite person.

Ms Woods had pursed her lips in a disapproving manner when Mr Tipett had exited the interview so quickly, but it wasn't until she chased after him to apologise that Freddie realised the pursed lips were for him.

"I'm not sure those questions were all very appropriate, Freddie," said his teacher later. "I applaud you for your tenacity, but really, we have to consider the reputation of the school as well. I don't want to lose the library either, but we can't just go around interrogating people in public positions like that."

"But Ms Woods, you gave us *permission* to interrogate, I mean, interview, him," said Freddie.

"Yes, well, I didn't realise it was going to pan out quite the way it did," said Ms Woods. "However, Mr Tipett told me on his way out that it was all OK, so we'll leave it at that."

Freddie knew, however, that Mr Tipett had been rightly rattled by his line of questioning and he was pleased. If Portsteven Library *was* going to close, then he and his friends certainly weren't going to let it happen without a fight.

***

Brain and Rob were staying over at Freddie's that night and they all took great pleasure in telling Mercury about the radio interview over dinner. Freddie's dad was still at the office.

"Well, I must say, it sounds like you did put the wind up the poor man," she said, smiling. "I'm glad to see that your father and I have raised a bit of a rebel, Fred! It's important to stand up and fight for causes you believe in. Peacefully, of course. Speaking of which, Laurel's organising our peaceful protest for Saturday morning. I'm afraid that we received an email from the LAB today and it wasn't very nice reading."

"What did it say, Mrs May?" asked Brain.

"It was just one of those padded-out emails, full of official jargon and whatnot, but essentially, informing us about the inspection's ongoing progress. There will be further updates but in the meantime they're reducing our opening hours." Mercury sighed. "They're worried about public money expenditure and so on. Load of old nonsense. What better use of public money than a free-to-use resource for the public?! Something for everyone of every age to enjoy and learn from and to socialise in … We'll just need to remind them of all that on Saturday. Well, I suppose my reduced working hours will give me more time to prep for the protest." She smiled, but there was no sun in it.

"We'll be there, mum!" said Freddie, waving his fork in the air. "With reinforcements."

"Yes, you can count on us, Mrs May," said Brain.

Rob, chewing seriously, nodded his agreement.

"That's wonderful to hear, boys. All support is very much appreciated. I just hope it will be enough. I suppose we aren't quite as busy as we once were, which is unfortunate, but we do have a healthy membership, despite that. And our books and fittings might have seen better days, but that doesn't mean they should close us down."

The rest of the evening was spent finishing homework and watching TV, before Freddie, Brain and Rob headed to bed. They were bubbling with excitement as Freddie was going to try summoning Meg again for another meeting. As far as they were concerned, midnight couldn't come quick enough.

***

While Freddie, Brain and Rob tackled their homework, Meg and the Book-Keepers of Thesaurus had work of their own to do – new, though not wholly unexpected work.

They were under attack.

The Book Worms had burrowed their way into the forest of firs which bordered Thesaurus and had been spotted by a look-out when they surfaced to feed on the trees. Winifred Thorne and the rest of the committee had already put out the call for Book-Keepers to assemble and fight back, but they needed as much help as they could get. Meg wondered if she should ask Freddie for help but decided he was probably busy enough in his own world, working on the plans he had with his friends there. And besides, he'd never faced a Book Worm in battle before, so what use would he really be? It soon became clear that they needed many more bodies to fight the Book Worms, however, so when she heard

Freddie's summons as he rapped out his message on the bookcase, she reconsidered.

Tonight called for all hands on deck.

***

At the witching hour, three boys huddled around the old bookcase in Freddie's room. Freddie had rapped the wood using a special knock he'd agreed with Meg at their last meeting and they waited in anticipation for her arrival.

They didn't have to wait long.

Brain and Rob stared in fascination as the outline of a door appeared, followed by the door opening and Meg popping her head around it. She looked a little pale, Freddie thought, but nevertheless, flashed them a grin.

"Can't stop long tonight, I'm afraid," she said, wincing. "Book Worm trouble."

"This is Brain and Rob," said Freddie, indicating his two friends. "We didn't really have time for proper introductions in the library last week."

Meg smiled at the boys, who nodded in return, both trying to suppress their excitement but betraying themselves with widened eyes and a sudden speechlessness.

"Good to meet you both," said Meg. "I'm afraid we don't really have much time to chat – again – but I was wondering if I could ask you all for a favour. I mean, it's probably not a good idea but, well, we're sort of desperate."

"What is it?" asked Freddie.

"Well, I was just going to ask if you three wanted to come and help us with the current Book Worm infestation in Thesaurus, but I'm not sure —"

"Of course we'll come!" Rob beamed.

Brain looked a little less sure but then nodded enthusiastically.

"Really?" Meg grinned. "I should warn you, though. It's kinda dangerous."

"We'll help you," said Freddie firmly. "Of course we will. Don't worry about us. Rob does karate and, er —"

"Yeah, we'll let Rob go ahead and karate-chop those worms, then we'll finish them off," said Brain, making sweeping motions with his hands in the air.

"Thanks, guys," said Rob, punching Brain in the arm good-naturedly.

"Great!" said Meg. "Well, if you're sure, then let's go. I'll explain the situation on the way." Without further discussion, she took her magic dust from a pouch slung around her waist and blew it into their eyes. Brain and Rob looked suitably startled when they all shrunk to Book-Keeper size within seconds.

Freddie grinned at them. "Now then. Let's go find those Book Worms."

Chapter Seventeen

How to Keep Yourself Alive

"So – here's how you keep yourself alive when you meet a Book Worm," said Meg, as she led them through the bookcase.

"Er, what?" said Brain, who seemed to have lost some of his bravado now they were actually on their way to help the Book-Keepers.

"Alive," said Meg, looking back at them over her shoulder with a grin. "You do *want* to stay alive, don't you?"

"Of course we do!" spluttered Brain. "But just how dangerous are these Book Worms anyway? Maybe I should have done some research before agreeing to this ..."

"Relax, Brain," said Freddie. "Meg's just winding us

up, right Meg? I mean, of course they're dangerous, but we'll be OK."

"If you listen to me you should be fine, but there's really no guarantee … OK, OK, I'm winding you up a *little*," said Meg, as Freddie threw her a look, "but you shouldn't underestimate a Book Worm and you won't find any information about them in your world as they're very much a species of ours."

"What do they look like?" asked Rob, who was bringing up the rear, behind Brain, with Freddie and Meg in front.

"Well, they're basically as they sound – giant worms," said Meg. "They start off small, like most creatures, but can grow to the size of, well, nobody really knows, as they just seem to keep on growing. They could be as big as a bus or as long as a river. It's really impossible to say."

"A ri-river?" said Brain. "That's massive! This is insane. Fred – I'm not so sure about this anymore."

They'd reached the end of the tunnel and stood looking at one another in silence for a few moments.

Meg spoke first. "OK, here's the situation. The outskirts of our town, which is called Thesaurus by the way, is being infested by Book Worms, but they haven't grown to the epic proportions I just described. Yet."

"Well, that's a relief," said Brain, visibly relaxing at the Book-Keeper's words.

"But they *could* grow huge and destroy the town and our library?" said Freddie.

"Yes." Meg nodded. "If we don't stop them they'll overrun Thesaurus and then eat their way through to your world."

"Eat?" Now Rob looked as peaky as Brain.

"They eat whatever gets in their way," said Meg. "They prefer books and bookish materials, but will devour anything or any*one* who tries to stop them doing what they like to do best. They'll go through the Travelling Tree and pop out in the libraries it leads to. Ordinarily, the threat of them is easier to keep on top of, but once libraries start decaying – closing down or risking closure and being destroyed – it seems to give them extra vigour and they come en masse to get in on the action and hasten the demise of the library in question. They're basically drawn to decay."

"I thought the doors in the Travelling Tree kept changing," said Freddie. "That they lead to so many different places the same door doesn't necessarily go to the library it did the last time it was used?"

"Yes, but its bark holds the memory of all the libraries we visit and the routes we take to reach them. That includes paths to some of the most famous and oldest libraries in the world. It would be catastrophic if the Book Worms attacked them. The scent of decaying or at-risk libraries like Portsteven Library would attract them to those trails and doorways first, as easy pickings, but they'd soon turn their attention to the others and then we'd really be in trouble.

"Book Worms prefer munching on weakened libraries, as they're more vulnerable and easier to destroy than healthy, well-protected ones. That means they can grow bigger much faster and become almost impossible to fight. So, when they go on to attack *healthy* libraries, they're even more of a force to be reckoned with. Anyway, going back to what I was saying before – here's how you keep yourself alive in the company of Book Worms."

The boys waited with bated breath for the answer. Meg gave them an uneasy smile.

"Number one – cut off their heads, if you can. Works

better the smaller they are. Number two – lead them to the river and hope they follow you in and drown. Number three – run. It won't kill them, obviously, but it might just save *you*. They move quickly, these worms. Don't underestimate them. Proper little – or large – racers they are. Now – questions?"

"Um, yes!" said Brain. "What are we going to see when you open that door? Are Book Worms going to come charging towards us? We don't even have any weapons!"

"Don't worry, we'll pick up some weaponry on the way through Thesaurus," said Meg. "Hopefully the Book Worms haven't reached town yet so, no, I don't expect to see any come charging at us when I open the door. But let's see, shall we?"

She tapped the wood, muttered a few words and it swung open.

***

Hallow was pleased.

Things were on track. They were going to *plan*. The Book-Keepers were distracted. The girl was too. The humans were ... interesting. Troublesome? Perhaps. But first – useful. They weren't to know. Pity them. Well, if pity was something Hallow went in for.

It wasn't.

Well, perhaps occasionally, he kept some pity aside for himself. No harm in that, was there? A little self-indulgence now and again in a world which had no place for him ... He shook himself. Now *he* was getting distracted.

Enough.

While the Book-Keepers were away, Hallow would play.

Actually, no.

Hallow would wreak havoc.

***

The breeze brought news to the Travelling Tree of what was unfolding elsewhere in Thesaurus. It wasn't good. The firs of the forest, some of them gnawed on and felled by greedy Book Worms, whispered their warnings to the air; their tangled roots thrummed and hummed as they too transmitted important information to the gargantuan tree through which Freddie and his friends had passed not so long ago.

The air rippled; the soil stirred; the trees spoke to the elements and between themselves as their community unravelled the real plan at hand.

In Thesaurus Square, the Travelling Tree listened. It caught the warning from the breeze in its paged leaves, listened to the news being relayed through the roots.

Someone was coming.

The Travelling Tree waited, still and outwardly silent, save for the rustlings of its bookish boughs, though inside, of course, it was full flow in communication – like it always was. The ancient, magical tree watched as Hallow – a shadow of a thing that was once destined to be a Book-Keeper and then veered off in another direction – crept into its woodwork. The Travelling Tree couldn't stop him, nor would it have, for all would happen as it must in order to reach a conclusion.

The story had to play out as it was meant to.

Hallow's flavour was like that of milk on the turn; it was spoiled berries and rotting vegetation; mulch and mayhem. And yet, the Travelling Tree knew that even rot and decay were vital for growth – for life. A dead tree, after all, teamed with all sorts of organisms – insects and fungi – and was crucial in feeding a healthy forest or wood.

Yes, rot had its own value. So, when Hallow requested entry across the Travelling Tree's threshold, there was no resistance at all.

The roots continued to hum and the air sang on.

Chapter Eighteen

Battle of the Book Worms

Almost expecting to see giant book-eating worms slithering about the place consuming bookish houses and Book-Keepers, despite what Meg said, Freddie was relieved when they stepped out into silence, with no worms in sight.

"Good," said Meg. "They haven't reached the Travelling Tree yet. Come on – we need to help the others."

None of them sensed the eyes in the shadows watching them go, as Freddie, Brain and Rob quickly followed Meg, taking a different route from Freddie's last visit. This time, she led them in the opposite direction, past more literary buildings which tapered out towards the boundary of Thesaurus, clearly defined by a forest of poker-straight firs. The trees towered above them like sentries, which Freddie supposed they were, in a way. He saw figures moving in amongst the evergreens, others working at the ground in front, and guessed that most of the town must be helping to banish the Book Worms.

"The problem is," puffed Meg, "the wretched things burrow underground and then pop up like moles in all sorts of places. The bigger they are the easier it is to spot their tunnelling, but when they're small to average-size, the job gets a lot trickier."

"What are those Book-Keepers doing?" asked Rob, as they reached the forest perimeter.

"Casting new protection spells on the earth, reinforcing the ones already in place to stop the worms and setting up alarms so we'll hear them coming if any Book Worms trigger them. The spells only go so deep, though, and worms can burrow further down into the soil than we think the magic can reach. But still, it all helps."

"What do you need us to do?" asked Brain.

"*We're* going into the forest to help get rid of some worms that have already slithered through it and are heading our way. It's better if they never reach these

146

defences, as the danger then is in them being breached."
Meg waved at the Book-Keepers they passed and they
waved back, then she led the boys into the cool darkness
of the forest.

The trees grew close together, their thick foliage
absorbing the sounds of life within, or so it seemed to
Freddie. Could you hear a Book Worm burrow, or slide
across the soil? He tried to remember from his last – and
only – encounter so far with the creatures and recalled a
sinister slithering sound. *Giant* Book Worms would
surely create even more noise. Or, perhaps, experience
would make them stealthier.

They followed Meg in single file, winding through
the trunks like their own peculiar version of worm, until
shouts pierced the silence like spears. They froze, then
bolted towards the commotion, cracking twigs and
other foliage underfoot.

Freddie gasped, branches scratching his face as they
fled onwards. The shouts grew louder. The trees
thinned a little and he heard water rushing as fast as the
blood in his veins. A river. It ran like an artery through
the forest, with trees on either side, banks sloping down
at a gentle gradient. On this side of the river, Freddie

saw a group of Book-Keepers grappling with something in the water. They must have caught a Book Worm. It thrashed ferociously, spray drenching the Book-Keepers as they battled. Freddie hadn't been prepared for how he would feel about the reality of worm warfare. They were obviously dangerous, as he trusted Meg's account, but he liked animals and couldn't bear to see them suffer. Book Worms might be on the other end of the lovable scale from puppies, or his favourite animals – tigers – but suffering was suffering, no matter the type of creature. He caught Meg by the arm.

"Isn't there a more humane way of dealing with the worms? Something less fatal? I mean, I know they're dangerous and have to be stopped, but — "

"Freddie, they'd eat us alive if we didn't kill them. And then they'd breed more of themselves to eat more of us and our – *your* – books and libraries. These are a whole other breed of worm – of creature. They don't deserve your sympathy," her eyes darkened, "or compassion."

They watched as a Book-Keeper swung silver and lopped off a white wormy head. It plopped into the water to the sound of cheers. The celebrations didn't last long, however. The river began bubbling like a witch's cauldron. More worms were coming.

"Quick," said Meg. "Grab anything you can. We have to stop them. Fred?"

Freddie swallowed, then nodded.

"I thought you said they weren't very big yet?" said Brain, his eyes widening as a string of worm heads broke the river's surface. They looked like giant buoys, bobbing on the water.

"Erm, they do grow quickly and it can be hard to guess their true size until they emerge from underground," said Meg. "Anyway, less talk and more fighting!"

"Wait a minute," Rob butted in. "Didn't you also say that we could keep ourselves alive by forcing them into a river? Well, they're already *in* the flipping river and they still look pretty dangerous to me! In fact, they seem quite happy to be there!"

"Not if you sit on their heads and drown them." Meg winked at a spluttering Rob as she darted to the riverbank.

Armed with sticks from the forest and wavering spirits, Freddie, Brain and Rob followed, none wishing to look like cowards, yet all wearing dubious, apprehensive expressions. Is this, Freddie wondered, what's meant when people talk about meeting your doom? He certainly hoped not. Thinking that a war cry might help his courage, he let out a roar as he ran and heard Brain and Rob do the same. Meg shot a bemused look over her shoulder but said nothing.

The Book-Keepers weren't having as much luck now with the worms. They were caught up in a mess of limbs and wormy white flesh and muddy water, which occasionally sprayed black when a worm's skin was sliced. Black-blooded beasts. Freddie shivered. He swung a stick blindly into the melee but it connected with nothing but air. Surely there were better ways they could be helping? He wasn't exactly sure that fighting killer worms was the best use of his skills.

He soon discovered, however, that battling for your life and other people's, wrapped up in fighting for a cause everyone believed in for the greater good, provided suitable ammunition in the form of unbridled energy and zeal. Letting the Book Worms win would be disastrous for everyone and so, Freddie and his friends fought as they literally never had before.

Freddie had no idea how many Book Worms were in the river, but as more and more Book-Keepers joined them, he started to hope they would beat the fiends down. He saw Meg swing at part of a worm – which part was anyone's guess – and saw more of that thick black blood ooze out. These were definitely no ordinary animals.

Brain and Rob were busy battling the tail-end of a worm the size of an elephant, while a cluster of Book-Keepers struggled with its head, which the creature swung from side-to-side, trying to dislodge a sprightly Book-Keeper who had clambered on top of it and was clinging to its thick neck. The Book-Keeper was flung into the air as the Book Worm flicked its head upwards, then promptly disappeared down the worm's throat. Freddie felt a chill spread through him. Around him, Book-Keepers screamed and a few seconds later, one of them hacked through the worm's neck and separated the head from its still writhing body.

Distracted by the grisly scene upriver, Freddie had frozen to the spot but was jolted out of his stupor by a gust of mulchy breath on his neck. He jumped and looked round into the scrunched-up face of a Book

Worm with ragged, razor teeth. Not giant-sized but certainly big enough to do him serious damage. He couldn't seem to move his limbs, though. What was wrong with him? He was about to get eaten by a giant Book Worm and all he could do was stand there.

"Freddie, look out!" yelled Rob, waving frantically at him.

Freddie shook his head and, just in time, remembered the stick in his hand. As the worm reared back, so too did Freddie's arm and he lobbed the piece of wood as hard as he could through the air, then turned and ran. He glanced back and saw the stick lodge in the Book Worm's jaws. The worm tried to shake it out, but it was stuck fast. In its distraction, it failed to notice a knot of approaching Book-Keepers and, before Freddie knew it, the worm and its companions were finally gone, the shouts had ebbed away and all that could be heard was the flow of the river and the giddy breaths of those who had survived. Which was most people, Freddie hoped, looking round at the dishevelled group. He searched for his friends and saw Meg hi-fiving Brain and Rob. He gave a sigh of relief.

From now on, his only participation in battles was

going to be reading about them in the pages of a book.

***

Hallow's journey through the Travelling Tree took almost no time at all. He felt it was a very efficient means of getting about. If only he could use it more often.

His battalion of Book Worms had served their purpose, otherwise he would have met with trouble upon his return to Thesaurus. He didn't mourn any that wouldn't return to him. As long as he had enough to see his plan through to the end.

The good thing was, Book Worms propagated quickly. In fact, the eggs he'd just planted in Portsteven Library should be hatching any … time … soon.

Chapter Nineteen

Interlude

As Freddie, Brain and Rob made their way back to the Travelling Tree with Meg, it started raining letters.

'M's and 'o's, along with 'a's, 'f's, 'h's and all the rest of the alphabet splish-splashed around them, to the boys' great amazement. Freddie opened his palm and a jumble of 'q's, 's's and 't's, along with an assortment of what looked like punctuation, splattered across his fingers.

Brain caught an 'm' on his tongue. "You know what," he said, grinning, "if it can rain letters then maybe, *somewhere*, it can actually really rain cats and dogs!"

"Yeah, and pigs might still fly," said Rob, rolling his eyes.

"Who says they can't – *some*where?" said Meg, arching an eyebrow. Rob looked at her, trying to work out if she was winding him up or not. Meg smiled smugly.

Now that the imminent Book Worm danger had passed, the townsfolk seemed to be getting back to their normal routine. Even though it was night-time, Thesaurus was buzzing with activity and everyone was in high spirits, thanks to their battle victory. The town twinkled with white fairy lights, the moon hanging round and full as a fortune-teller's crystal ball. Chattering voices and outbursts of laughter coloured the air as relief spread through the Book-Keeper community.

"Do you think there'll be more Book Worms?" Freddie asked Meg.

She frowned. "There'll be more where those came from, I'm pretty sure of that, but hopefully tonight will buy us some time. They won't give up trying to force their way through to the Travelling Tree though, when they sense that Portsteven Library is ripe for the picking. That's why it's important we save it – and quickly. When's your protest taking place again?"

"This Saturday," said Freddie. "We're meeting Gwen and Graham after school tomorrow so we can find out how their research on Mr Tipett has been going and what else they've been up to. Don't worry, we'll do our best to stop him from closing the library. My dad's already agreed to cover the protest in his newspaper, and ..." Freddie paused as an idea flashed into his head. "We record all of our interviews for the school radio, so maybe we could 'accidentally' leak Tipett's interview to the local radio station."

"But they'd know it was us, Fred," said Brain. "I'd say that if your dad does a story then the rest of the media will soon come knocking on old Tipett's door anyway."

"Yeah, I suppose so," said Freddie. "Hopefully, he won't know what's hit him."

"Good," said Meg. "We'll keep on with our defence tactics here, against the Book Worms, while you're busy with all of that. Portsteven needs to be a healthy library, safe from closure and protected by the community, if we want to get rid of those dratted worms."

"Don't worry," said Freddie. "We're on it!"

They really needed to get back home, as it was late

and there was always the chance that Freddie's parents might look in on the boys to check they were sleeping and not still awake on a school night, but even so, battling Book Worms was hungry work and they couldn't resist stopping to sample some of the lovely-smelling feast that was appearing around them.

Book-Keepers were spilling out into the street and congregating around the Travelling Tree, celebrating their victory, and with them came all manner of enticing aromas, which trailed out of doors and windows to tempt the hungry group.

"Margot!" Meg waved at a willowy Book-Keeper wearing a red silk robe stitched with golden dragons. "You don't mind if we have a few for the road?" She pointed at the food the woman was arranging on a long table, where other Book-Keepers were also putting out refreshments.

Margot, whose hair was as black as a raven, beckoned them over. "Of course – help yourselves. Are you going to introduce me to your friends?"

Meg grabbed a muffin, took a bite and swallowed. "Thanks. This is Freddie, Brain and Rob – from beyond the bookcase. They're helping us save Portsteven

Library and came tonight to help fight the Book Worms too."

"Pleased to meet you," said Margot. "I'm Meg's mother, by the way. I'm glad to hear that you young fellows are so dedicated to protecting books and their guardians. Libraries are like an Aladdin's Cave, don't you think? Full to the brim of treasures and journeys and all sorts of colourful characters. They house hope and thought and adventure ... oh, and so much more besides. They're treasure houses. Sanctuaries for studying. Everyone should have a library they can use – they will enrich their lives on every visit!"

"My mum's head librarian at our library in Portsteven," said Freddie, munching a muffin which tasted of summer berries and vanilla.

"How absolutely wonderful!" said Margot, clapping her hands together. "A fellow guardian. She would be delighted to know that you're assisting us Book-Keepers in saving it, though she mustn't discover that, of course. Adults just can't fathom us, really. We only ever communicate with the children and only then when we really *need* to. I wish you luck with everything. In the meantime, we'll be doing our best back here to stop those Book Worms."

"Thanks," said Freddie.

"Come on – we'd better be off," said Meg. "See you later, mum."

They waved their goodbyes, then pressed through the jumble of Book-Keepers' bodies to the Travelling Tree.

"Er, why do you call your mum, Margot?" asked Rob.

"Because it's her name, of course!" said Meg with a grin. "I call her 'mum' too, but it's just something we do here. Kids mostly call their parents by their given names. Is that so strange?" She laughed at the bemused look on Rob's face.

When they reached the Travelling Tree Brain paused before stepping through the doorway that would return them to Freddie's house. "Do you think we'll ever be back here? Or remember all this when we're grown-ups?"

"I don't know," said Freddie. "I hope so."

"Maybe if we look after stories and keep telling them and reading them and celebrating them, we'll always remember their magic and the possibilities they create," said Brain. "And we'll remember our own exciting – and not so exciting – stories and won't forget that we lived them. Maybe. Gwen never forgot about the Book-Keepers, after all, and she's *really* old now."

"We are masters of our own minds!" declared Rob, throwing his arm into the air like a sword.

Meg watched them in amusement. "Yeah, well, when you're done philosophising, guys, I think it's time we stepped on it and got you home. If you want something to really get you thinking, though, then how about this. Do you think dreams are just dreams, or do you think that, actually, when you sleep, those stories keep on flowing and sweep the unconscious you up into another world that wide-awake you will never access? The question is, which world is the more real? The one in which you're awake, or asleep?"

Brain's eyes looked ready to pop from concentration and Rob slapped his forehead. "Way to fry a brain, Ms Book-Keeper," he said. "Let's get outta here. That's a whole bunch of thoughts for a whole other day."

Chapter Twenty

Scandal

Freddie, Brain and Rob rose from bed with some difficulty the next morning, after their adventures with Meg. They ate a hurried breakfast once Mercury finally dragged the covers from the beds to rouse them, after repeated failed attempts to summon them downstairs.

"I thought I told you three not to be up all night talking?" she said, as they crunched toast and slurped orange juice on their way out the door. "You'd better stay awake at school today!"

That, as it turned out, was quite a task, as Freddie, Brain and Rob could hardly keep their eyes open all day, particularly in the boring bits of their lessons. However, as the clock ticked on towards home-time, their energy levels seemed to mysteriously grow and by the time they left school for the library, they felt almost back to normal again. Gwen was waiting for them when they arrived and waved vigorously. She was as eye-catching as a ladybird among ants, however, so Freddie didn't think the waving was really necessary.

Settled in their secluded corner, the five wasted little time in catching up. The table was strewn with books to keep up the pretence of their book club and their discussion *did* focus on books, so Freddie didn't feel too guilty about the subterfuge. His mother had smiled brightly at him when they came in and seemed to approve of their new mixed age bookish gathering.

After filling Gwen and Graham in on their Book Worm battle (with much oohing and ahhing from Gwen and quiet contemplation from Graham), they asked the Silver Surfers what they'd uncovered about Mr Tipett.

"Well, now, *there's* a story," said Gwen conspiratorially. She lowered her voice even further so they all had to lean in towards her to catch the words. "Turns out, my boys, that Mr Tipett has a bit of a shady history. Our deep-dive internet search revealed a few interesting facts about 'the enemy'." She narrowed her eyes and pursed her lips.

"Like what?" asked Rob.

"Like ... the fact he has *form* when it comes to matters involving books." She shook her head in disgust.

"Matters? What matters?" said Freddie, wishing she would get to the point a little more quickly.

"It seems our Mr Tipett was involved in closing down another library when he was in his last job. *And* he was quite vocal about removing the English department from that town's university – and was no doubt instrumental in its demise. It's all there in the online newspaper reports, if you dig back a few years. It looks like Mr Tipett has an unpleasant appetite for destroying, removing and/or preventing any sort of bookish establishments from putting down roots.

"He only recently became a LAB board member but he hasn't wasted any time in trying to sabotage its good work with local libraries. As a writer and a reader I am outraged at this snivelling little man's behaviour! We're still digging, aren't we Graham?" Graham nodded. "And I wouldn't be surprised if we found out he was a thwarted writer himself. Maybe his parents never read to him when he was a boy. Who knows the reasons behind such despicable behaviour? He moves around from place to place, weeding out bookish havens and trying, often successfully, to shut them down."

"He sounds exactly like a Book Worm in human form," said Freddie.

Gwen's eyes widened. "Now *there's* a possibility! Maybe he's an informant! That's something to check with your young Book-Keeper friend, boys. Do Book Worms shapeshift and do they have people out here working for them?"

"Don't know if they'd be clever enough to have a network of informants," said Brain dubiously. "They're just big worms, in the end."

"Hmm ... an OCG (that's Organised Crime Group, boys) staffed by Book Worms with a human – or human-*like* – leader living amongst us. Never rule out the seemingly impossible – you just don't know what the universe might throw at you!"

"I thought old people were supposed to have more sense," muttered Rob.

"Who told you that?" Gwen's sharp ears didn't miss a syllable. "Stuff and nonsense, I say. No, as you grow older, boys, you often find that you revert back to your childhood self, who's simply been slumbering in the background, waiting for you to break free from the mundane world of work responsibilities and throw it all off to embrace the wilderness of retirement.

"At our age, we've seen and done enough not to care about most things anymore and we know something of the absurdity of the world. We revel in our re-won freedom and allow our inner youthful imaginations to flourish once more. It's why so many of us become rather good writers and creatives in our old age.

"Anyway," Gwen glanced at each of them in turn around the table. "As the peaceful protest is taking place this Saturday morning, we need to get busy with organising placards, posters and soundbites. You'll know all about those, young Freddie, what with your father being a journalist.

"We have to make sure his newspaper gives the story as much coverage as it can – and get the local radio station and any other media involved too. Lots to do, boys!"

There was indeed much to keep them busy, as Freddie, Brain and Rob had homework to do on top of all Gwen's tasks. With just two days to go until the weekend, Freddie guessed they wouldn't have a minute to spare.

Chapter Twenty-one

Save Our Library

The next two days were very busy indeed for the boys – and for Meg, who joined them at Freddie's house in the evenings when they were making their placards. After homework, of course. Freddie had designed one which said, *'Save our library!'* He thought it was simple but effective, though he added in some pictures of books around the edges, just to drive home the point.

Brain's sign read, *'Love your library? Save Portsteven's!'* while Rob's said, *'Knowledge should be free – we need our library!'*

"Rhymes," he said with a smug smile.

"Yes, how eloquent of you," said Brain, rolling his eyes.

Rob shoved him playfully. "The world needs its

poets!"

"Hmm, but whoever thought that would translate as *you*?"

Freddie laughed. "Laurel'll like it. She'll love them all. I wonder how Gwen and Graham are getting on with theirs?"

They'd agreed to meet the Silver Surfers on the morning of the protest and skip their after-school library visits on Thursday and Friday, as Gwen wanted to spread the word in person as much as she could before then.

"We need to make sure there's a *big* crowd on Saturday," she'd said. "We have to make some noise and get their attention. Lots of people don't know the protest is even happening. *And,* hopefully when a crowd gathers, more people will see us and join in."

Freddie had already asked his dad about giving the protest full coverage in his newspaper and he'd readily agreed.

"Fantastic, Freddie. If you get a big enough crowd and our photographer an impressive picture, then this could make the splash."

"You mean, we could be on the front page? That'd be

great, dad." Freddie knew the splash was the most coveted position in any newspaper and it would certainly give them the attention they wanted. No one would miss hearing about Portsteven Library's predicament if they were on that!

"You could indeed, Fred. It's an important local news story. If we don't draw attention to these sorts of things they just disappear under the radar, but make enough noise and you never know what might happen."

"Your namesake was often in the newspaper too, Fred," said Mercury with a grin. "See, you're just like him, after all. Well ..." She exchanged one of those 'adult looks' as Freddie called them, with his dad. "I mean, you'll be in the paper for a different reason, but still. Similarities. You're creating a bit of a stir and that's good. Standing up for what you believe in will always be supported in this house."

"Hear, hear!" said Freddie's dad.

By the time Saturday rolled around Freddie was buzzing with excitement. Laurel had called in with his mum before heading to the library. She beamed at him as he came into the kitchen, her silver bob bouncing as she rushed over to hug him. She was around the same age as his mum but Laurel liked to follow unusual trends and, after spotting a few "prematurely grey hairs," had decided to try out the look currently being worn by "the young models" and go full-on metallic. "It's all the rage these days," she'd insisted. "And it means it won't come as such a shock to me when I finally turn a completely natural grey later on."

"Morning, Fred," she said now. "Are you looking forward to today? It's a big day for all us bookworms, literature lovers and supporters of open access to learning! Not to mention social inclusion, upskilling and basic human rights!"

"Er, yes," said Freddie, his voice muffled by Laurel's layers of colourful clothing. "Dad's doing a story on it too—"

"Oh, I know! Mercury told me. It'll help a great deal, let me tell you. Never underestimate the power of publicity! The importance of words on paper – that's what this is all about, after all."

Once everyone was ready, they all drove down to Portsteven Library together, Freddie's father included.

"Solidarity is important in these sort of circumstances," he said. "And I'm an editor who likes to keep his hand in when it comes to writing stories – especially those involving my own family."

Freddie wondered what his dad would say if he knew the *real* 'whole story' – of Book Worms as they existed in Thesaurus and of the secretive Book-Keepers who acted as guardians for the many libraries around the world. It would no doubt make a much juicier story and sell more newspapers, but he knew another thing that was important in 'these sort of circumstances' – protecting your sources at all costs and abiding by the unwritten rules Meg had told him about.

Magical universes were best kept secret from adults.

***

Meanwhile, in a handful of dark corners in Portsteven Library, tucked out of sight at the backs of bookcase shelves, something munched.

More than one something.

Pages were nibbled, then torn by tiny teeth, for Book Worms were no ordinary worms – they had their own ammunition. They worked quickly, shifting their attention between books and bookcases, for the wood delighted them in different ways than the tomes they held. These babies wouldn't stay as such for long, as they'd been planted in a nursery where they could really do nothing but thrive.

Chapter Twenty-two
Peaceful Protest

As morning stretched and settled in around them, Portsteven Library got dressed for the protest. Cold pinched their cheeks but the weather forecaster on the radio promised a dry day and already, a primrose sun was peeping out from behind the clouds.

Freddie, Brain and Rob tied colourful balloons to the doors and inside the library, while Mercury and Laurel hung a banner across the entrance which proclaimed: *'Love your library? Help us save it!'* Refreshments were set up in the foyer with tea, coffee and hot chocolate, as well as scones and pastries from The Painted Pot. Freddie knew that sandwiches were waiting in the staff kitchen, with chocolate biscuits for later too. Really, the protest had more of a party atmosphere to it than anything else, which only grew as more and more people started arriving to add their support. Initially, these were friends of Laurel and Mercury but soon, Freddie recognised other regular library users and some people from school too, Ms Woods amongst them. Gwen and Graham arrived with a group of Silver Surfers which had swollen in number.

"Friends and extended acquaintances," said Gwen with a knowing smile, as she bit into a scone and helped herself to coffee. "We'll just fuel up and then station ourselves outside for a while. Draw in some passers-by." She nodded at the door. "We've a few setting up deckchairs for those whose old legs won't stand the strain." She chuckled. "Which is most of us!"

Freddie grinned. He wondered what it would be like to have creaky joints and brittle bones like the Silver Surfers and decided right there and then to never grow as old as Gwen and Graham. He was quite happy being young and didn't think he'd suit having slow-moving muscles and tired old limbs.

Laurel had taken charge of the crowd and was explaining how the protest would work. "We're peaceful people," she said firmly. "So no unruliness please. We want to present a united front of civilised protestors who understand the value of their local library and are determined to save it and make that publicly known. So, warm up with some hot beverages and then, out we go! Oh, and don't forget to smile for the cameras!"

"Wise words," whispered Gwen. "But why is that young woman's hair completely *grey*?"

Freddie, Brain and Rob exchanged grins as she shuffled off with the other Silver Surfers, some of whom actually had hair tinged with blue and purplely-pink.

"Right," said Freddie, picking up his placard. "Let's get outside and make some noise."

***

As the morning wore on and the number of protestors swelled, Freddie felt at last that they really could save the library. Surely all these people meant something? Surely their voices wouldn't go unheard? As Laurel led a chant which included the phrase, 'power to the people,' he was confident they would win. It was strange seeing people from different parts of his life all jostling together for a common cause. His mum mingled with his classmates, his teacher with his dentist, his newfound Silver Surfer friends with his dad … Really, it was all a bit bizarre, in a way, but the mood was upbeat and it felt uplifting and more and more normal by the minute.

Mercury had been persuaded to do an interview with the local radio station, the reporter nodding seriously as she mentioned 'cuts' and described the library as a 'sanctuary for study and learning'. After a few seconds of looking nervous at all the attention, she seemed to take it in her stride and spoke clearly and confidently into any microphone or dictaphone thrust in front of her, Freddie's father nodding encouragingly and scribbling down his own notes for the newspaper article. Press photographers flashed their cameras and protestors and onlookers alike took pictures on their phones.

Yes, Freddie was sure they were making the right sort of noise to save Portsteven Library. Even the weather continued to favour them, throwing watery sunlight but no rain onto the crowd. It was cold but there was no biting wind, so it was perfectly bearable, especially if you paraded energetically up and down in front of the library waving your placards, like he was doing with Brain and Rob. In fact, Freddie was actually sweating.

The thing was, as well, that Freddie realised he now really wanted to save the library for the library's sake. He still wanted to protect his mum's job and make sure everyone could use it and, of course, he still wanted to help Meg and the Book-Keepers, but now he wanted to save the library because he was beginning to really appreciate how brilliant books were and how fantastic it was to be able to borrow them at any time from the library for free. His parents had always encouraged him to read, but hadn't forced him in case it put him off books completely. Mercury had always told her son that when the time was right, he'd discover the power of stories by himself (perhaps with a gentle nudge along the way). Well, it hadn't been quite the nudge he'd expected, but Freddie had most definitely discovered that books were worth reading. He wasn't going to let anyone steal his library now, just when he was becoming a bookworm, though thankfully not the kind the Book-Keepers were used to.

His neck prickled and he turned. It was as if his enemy had heard what he was thinking and had turned up just at that moment to quash all their hopes, for there, at last, stood Mr Tipett.

Chapter Twenty-three
Prom Parade

To the untrained eye, Mr Tipett looked quite calm as he surveyed the peaceful protest, but Freddie saw the thunderstorm in his eyes. His glasses only seemed to highlight it.

"Hello, young—" Mr Tipett left the sentence hanging like a hook. He knew Freddie's name but obviously didn't want Freddie to think he mattered enough for it to be remembered. Freddie decided to say nothing. Instead, he waited.

"Yes, well, how's my young interviewer today then?" said Mr Tipett. "You and your friends have certainly been busy since we spoke. Is, er, your mother about? Oh …" Relief fluttered over his face. "There she is. I must speak with her immediately. Nice, er, talking to you."

Mr Tipett narrowed his eyes at Freddie then turned on his heel and strode towards Mercury. Freddie released a breath he hadn't realised he'd been holding. He really hoped Mr Tipett wasn't going to create trouble but he didn't think he was here to show support. He waved Gwen over.

"Everything OK, Freddie?" she asked, glancing with a keen eye in Mr Tipett's direction.

"Mr Tipett's here," he hissed. "What'll we do now?" His sweat was quickly cooling.

"Oh, the man himself has shown up then, has he? Humpf. Well, he can't *do* anything today, so don't worry about that. We've got every right to exercise our views and to do so peacefully on library premises. Although, Laurel's talking about going on a parade down the prom, which I think is a rather splendid idea, don't you?"

"It'd make a great photo for the paper!" said Rob, who was listening in.

"And let even more people know what's happening," said Brain.

"I think I should maybe go and rescue mum first," said Freddie.

Mercury looked as if she was both listening to whatever Mr Tipett was saying while also trying desperately to get away from him. Freddie was just about to head over to her when he saw his dad approaching the pair. He had obviously had the same idea as his son.

"I must go and introduce myself, boys," said Gwen sweetly. "Get a personal grasp of this Mr Tipett. I'd like a word with your father too, Freddie – I want to make sure he grills Mr Tipett about his book-hating past!"

The Silver Surfer shuffled off and Freddie turned to Brain and Rob. "Street march?" They grinned and went to find Laurel.

***

The prom parade went rather well, in Freddie's opinion, with passers-by cheering them on and cars honking their support. They walked all the way down to the harbour and back and even one of the local community policemen told them they were doing a good job.

"My kids love reading," he told Laurel. "The missus too. She's up half the night devouring thrillers and whatnot. Don't know where we'd be without the library. I don't think our salaries could support the family's book habit if it disappeared!"

Comments like that broadened Laurel's smile and made her march even more energetically alongside her peaceful protestors. A few local authors Freddie hadn't heard of (probably because they wrote adult books) also joined in the march, so that by the time they returned to the library, they had somewhat grown in number.

"Gracious," said Mercury when she welcomed them all back. "You *have* been busy drumming up support. Thanks everyone. There's more sandwiches and tray bakes inside, if anyone's peckish; tea, coffee and hot chocolate too!" She flashed Freddie a smile before she was sucked back into the melee.

"Boys!"

Freddie, Brain and Rob turned to see Gwen and Graham coming towards them. Gwen had a glint in her eye, while Graham maintained his usual stoical appearance. Freddie wondered if he'd been a WW2 spy in a former life. He looked old enough and he certainly gave nothing away, being as silent as Gwen was vocal. They were like opposite sides of the same coin, both quite different from one another but with enough in common to unite them nevertheless.

"What is it?" he asked, as Gwen gathered them into a circle.

"We've unearthed some more tasty titbits about our Mr Tipett, that's what," she said triumphantly. "It seems he told your mother, Freddie, that his inspection results show evidence that Portsteven Library is too rundown and too seldom used to be – and I quote," she made air quotes with her fingers, "*financially viable*. He says nobody reads books anymore! Piffle! Did you ever hear the like of it? Yes, it's a wee bit shabby around the edges – though it's more what I would call lived-in – but you only have to look around you today to get an idea of how much people love it. Mercury says she has records that will prove Tipett otherwise – she has a register of all library members which shows how often they use the library, so you know what that makes me think?" She looked at them expectantly.

"Er, what?" asked Rob.

"It makes me think that Mr Tipett has," Gwen lowered her voice to a whisper, "*faked* his figures! Which means —"

"He's an old crook!" said Rob, beaming.

"Shh," hissed Gwen. "He might still be loitering about like a bad smell. We don't want him to know we're on to him."

"I think after our school radio interview he might already have an inkling," said Brain, glancing around as if he expected Mr Tipett to jump out at him at any moment.

"Well, that he might, but we don't need to go announcing it to him," said Gwen. "Now, once the news story is published in tomorrow's – no, wait, tomorrow's Sunday; it'll be in Monday's edition. Well, once it's printed on Monday we can see how old Tipett takes the news, as it were." She sniffed. "With all the interviews from library members and your mother, along with her *official* facts and figures – not to mention today's protest – well, I don't see how the Library Administration Body can fail to keep the library open! In fact, I'd like to think they'd be clamouring to pay for its upgrade. They should be ashamed of themselves for not looking after it better. Mercury does her best but she can only work with what she's got, after all."

Freddie shared Gwen's thoughts but he couldn't help

wondering if it would all really go to plan as the Silver Surfer said. Somehow, he didn't think Mr Tipett would give up without a fight.

***

Mr Tipett was *not* going to give up without a fight. He stalked away from the so-called peaceful protest with his head held high. How dare those bookish people make such a spectacle of themselves in front of the library – and down the prom, too! Well, they could think again if they thought this was going to have any positive effect on his final report.

Granted, he'd spoken again to the head librarian and she'd been quite civil to him, but there was a steeliness in her eyes that he didn't like – and her husband was a journalist, of all things! Now this was going to be all over the papers and on the radio, too. A proper, public broadcast this time. It was all getting a bit out of hand. It wasn't usually like this. Usually, people just meekly accepted what Mr Tipett said and waved goodbye to their libraries and bookshops. This was what he was good at, so what was he doing wrong this time?

It was all the fault of that flaming flame-haired boy – that was what. The librarian and journalist's son. He seemed to be friends with that nosey old woman with the walking stick, too. They were all clubbing together against him and he wasn't going to have it.

The first thing Mr Tipett was going to do was call up that newspaper and make sure the story didn't get published on Monday. The librarian's husband might be a journalist but he wasn't the editor, was he? Ha! That would teach them!

***

Back in his office Mr Tipett slammed the phone down. Flaming family of troublemakers. They could have told him the journalist *was* the editor of the newspaper!

Well, that was that then. Time to think of something else.

Chapter Twenty-four

Read All About It!

Bookworms lobby for library!

Peaceful protestors say 'no' to axing precious community hub

By Martin May: Editor-in-chief

LOCAL readers turned out in force on Saturday to protest against the potential closure of Portsteven Library.

The event was organised after a recent Library Administration Body (LAB) inspection hinted that the library could be line for more than just cuts and may actually be at risk of shutting down permanently. The news comes hot on the heels of the facility's reduced opening hours, which came into force last week.

Laurel Been, who led the protest with the full

support of head librarian, Mercury May, said it was unthinkable that the LAB could be considering closure of such a vital community resource.

"So many of our community use the library – for reading, researching, learning about the internet and much more," she said. "There's a book club, a Silver Surfers group and even a knitting group. Schools visit for book-related events and inside there's everything from computers and e-books, to audio books, newspapers and, of course, good old paperbacks. It's an important educational and social resource for everyone in the community and it's FREE. It's the heartbeat of our town and we just can't afford to lose it!"

Ms Been added that Saturday's protest had been organised to alert members of the public about the library's precarious future and to garner further support.

"We also wanted to show, in physical form, just how many people care about and use the library," she added. "We now ask the Library Administration Body and its inspectors to have another look at their report and the library itself, and then reconsider their next move."

LAB inspection

The man behind the LAB's library inspection is Mr Timothy Tipett, who told this newspaper that he couldn't possibly comment on the status of Portsteven Library while the inspection was ongoing. He did say, however, that it was his belief most people simply didn't read anymore and that showing up to demonstrate on Saturday didn't necessarily prove anything.

"Most of these people probably don't even use the library," he said. "They might be members – or they might not – but how many of them actually step inside the library and borrow books regularly, or are part of these in-house clubs?

"We also have to consider other elements, such as the general state of the library and how financially viable it is to maintain it."

'Silver Surfers' unite

One such member of Portsteven Library is Gwendoline Glass, an active participant in various library activities who is also a 'Silver Surfer' – a term used to refer to those senior citizens who are learning how to use the internet.

"Myself and many others use the library frequently," she said. "We borrow books in large print, as they're easier for us to read and are only available in libraries. I also like listening to audio books and my friend Graham and I are learning online skills in the Silver Surfers Club, which we just couldn't do if there wasn't a library. We're pensioners who can't afford to buy expensive computers and we weren't taught how to use them because they weren't invented when we were at school!

"We need to keep the library open so that everyone has access to all these wonderful free resources, which have such a positive impact on people's lives."

Portsteven Library 'very healthy'

Head librarian at Portsteven Library, Mercury May, said the peaceful protest on Saturday had been a huge success and that she was heartened by how many people, like Gwendoline,

had turned out to show their support.

"It really means a lot," she said. "My son and his friends were there, along with other pupils from their school. There were lots of our library members and other people from the community too. We even had quite a few new membership sign-ups on the day, which was great!"

Mrs May said she was convinced there were more people than ever enjoying the pleasures of reading in the town and she encouraged anyone who hadn't yet visited the library to come along.

"We're all very friendly and there are lots of resources, as well as books, available," she said. "Even if you just want a quiet space to sit for a while and read the newspaper, we have that too. We're here for everyone in the community and we'll do our best to make sure it stays that way.

"I'm not sure where Mr Tipett's data is coming from about library usage but I know from my own up-to-date records that Portsteven Library is a very healthy one!"

Public consultation pending?

The final LAB report, which will ultimately determine the future of Portsteven Library, is still pending publication, so it remains to be seen what the outcome of this saga will be.

A spokesperson from the government-funded organisation told this newspaper: "We can't comment on the library report until the final inspection is completed and the findings analysed in full. It may be that the decision is put out for public consultation at a later date. We ask that members of the public remain vigilant and await further details as we have them."

What next for book-lovers?

With the future of Portsteven Library hanging in the balance, only time will tell whether it's still here this time next year. Judging by Saturday's show of support for the facility, however, it seems that until then, the Portsteven community will keep on fighting. "Every town needs a library," said Silver Surfer, Gwen. "And we're going to do everything in our power to make sure we don't lose ours!"

Chapter Twenty-five

Plots and Plans

"Well, your dad's done a great job with the newspaper story," said Meg on Monday night, as she crouched over the columns, reading. "This is fantastic, Freddie. And the protest, too. Any word from Mr Tipett since?"

"Not yet," said Freddie. "I think we just have to wait for the LAB's report to come out now, but based on what he told my mum on Saturday, I don't think it'll be good …"

Meg frowned. "Well, we're managing to hold off the Book Worms – for now, anyway. I think the success of Saturday and of *this*," she poked at the newspaper, "has helped a lot. It's the magic of hope and positive action and it really *means* something."

"I'm glad," said Freddie, "but I can't help thinking – what if it's all been for nothing? If Tipett's bad report, false or not, makes the council close the library, then how can we fight *that*?"

Meg thought for a minute. Then she jumped up with a grin on her face. "Maybe that's just it, Freddie! Maybe we *don't* fight!"

"Huh? You've completely lost me now. Isn't that the whole point of all this? Fight to save the library? Otherwise, how can we win?"

"By *stealth* and persuasion, Freddie," said Meg mysteriously. She saw the look on Freddie's face and added, "OK, let me explain. We – I mean, *you* – have made everyone aware of the library's plight and that's great, but it's had no perceivable effect on old Tipett yet, am I right?"

"Right." Freddie nodded.

"So … We don't try to fight him and make him even more defensive. You tried confronting him already in the radio interview and it only raised his hackles, right?"

Freddie nodded again. He wasn't sure where exactly Meg was going with this.

"Well, the only other way is to try and make him see sense by *reasoning* with him, befriending him – showing him the power of stories and letting him see for himself just why we need to save the library."

"And we do that how, exactly? By inviting him round for tea? I don't think he'd come and I don't think my mum would have him in the house. In fact, I'm certain she wouldn't."

"Ha! No, I think we need to invite him to a place so full of stories that he can't *not* be won over by them."

"Wait a minute. Surely you don't mean ..?" Freddie stared at Meg, who squared her shoulders and stared straight back at him.

"Yes, I think drastic measures are called for, Freddie. If Mr Tipett holds the keys to the library's future, then we *must* make him a lover of books, libraries, bookshops and stories before the report is published. We don't have very much time left, so there's only one thing for it. We'll have to take Mr Tipett to the Story Forest."

***

Freddie filled Brain and Rob in on their plan the next

day at school. Brain looked dubious at the very idea but Rob was more optimistic about it all. Freddie soon discovered why.

"Can we all come?" his friend asked enthusiastically. "I'd love to see this Story Forest! You might make bookworms out of me and Brain here too." He grinned. "Well, not Book Worms like those ugly, slimy things, but proper human bookworms."

"You mean readers?" said Freddie, raising an eyebrow.

"Yes! Won't Ms Woods be pleased if we all turn into readers?"

"Speak for yourself, Rob," said Brain. "I already *do* read—"

"Yeah, books on space and science—"

"Still books!"

"But not novels like Fred's been reading recently."

Freddie felt his cheeks warm. "I haven't read that many," he mumbled. "Haven't had time, but yeah, the books I *have* read have been great – full of adventure and exploring."

"We could even write our own stories after all this library business," said Rob. "But we *won't*," he added, as Freddie frowned, "because we're sworn to secrecy about the Book-Keepers." He pulled his fingers across his mouth. "Lips zipped. But can we come, seriously?"

"I don't see why not," said Freddie. "Meg didn't say you couldn't and you've already been in the Book-Keepers' world, anyway."

"Gwen and Graham will want to come too," said Brain. "Well, Gwen will, anyway."

"I think she should, if she's able," said Freddie. "She met a Book-Keeper once before, after all, and she's kept their secret all these years. She loves books so much it'd be a shame for her not to see the Story Forest. We'd be better as a group, anyway. Strength in numbers. Extra brain power. We'll tell her about it this afternoon at the library."

Gwen, of course, was delighted at the thought of visiting the Story Forest and clapped her hands in glee at the prospect. Graham, however, wasn't with her that afternoon.

"He's come down with a bit of a cold, poor thing," said Gwen. "Probably stood out in the fresh air for too long on Saturday. He'll be OK, though; he just needs some rest and lots of warm brews and he'll be right as rain in no time. He's glad he's done his bit, so don't you worry about that. Now, let's talk Tipett."

They spent the rest of the afternoon discussing how to get Mr Tipett alone in the local bookshop. Meg had suggested a second-hand one might be better as it would likely be quieter and all the old books would help boost her magic, as they'd be accessing the Story Forest through the Travelling Tree this time, which was a little trickier than the less direct route she and Freddie had used before. She hadn't told the other Book-Keepers what they were planning, as it was forbidden to invite adults into their world, especially a book-hating adult who was trying to close a library. The Book-Keepers would be aghast if they knew Mr Tipett was going to visit such a sacred place as the Story Forest. Also, what if it didn't work as they hoped it would? What if Tipett couldn't be turned? Better that no one else know what they were planning, in case nothing came of it.

Mercury kept throwing them bemused glances but she was getting used to seeing them all hanging out together now and she was glad, Freddie knew, that he was taking such an interest in the library and in books. Unbeknown to Freddie, however, his mother had other things on her mind. Nibbled books, to be precise, and a possible infestation of mice. It was the last thing she needed in their current situation, so wondering what Freddie and his friends were whispering about so clandestinely was the least of her worries right now.

It was Gwen who told them how they could get Mr Tipett alone.

"Every Saturday morning he comes for a coffee – by himself – at The Painted Pot," she said. "Penny says he's like clockwork. A black coffee —"

"Black like his soul …" said Rob, with a grin.

"And a plain scone at 10am. On the dot. He's punctual, our Mr Tipett. Then he takes a stroll around the shops. So, we just have to make sure he wanders into The Leaning Stack bookshop this weekend – and hope the report isn't published before he does!"

Chapter Twenty-six

Play the Game

The rest of the week trailed past as Freddie and his friends counted down the days until Saturday. They had some good news midweek when Mercury told Freddie she'd received an email from the LAB telling her the report wouldn't be published for another few weeks.

"These things take time, you see. They have to be written and edited and pored over and checked by multiple eyes before they can be signed off for public viewing. Although, I do think Mr Tipett doesn't mind drawing out the process. I think he's taking a sort of sadistic pleasure in all of this and watching us squirm."

"You never know, mum. He might have a change of heart and write a more positive report than you're expecting," said Freddie, trying to cheer Mercury up and give her something to hope for.

"You have such a positive attitude, Fred, and I'm glad." She patted his cheek. "But I think we have to prepare ourselves for the worst, while hoping for the best ... I just pray he doesn't get wind of the mouse problem."

"What mouse problem?"

"Oh, nothing to worry about – I hope. It's just that I've been finding books with pages nibbled and even torn out. Some bookcases have been gnawed at, too. I suppose that's the problem with having old wooden ones. It attracts mice. Anyway, I'm on the case!"

Freddie might have thought nothing more of 'the mouse problem' if Mercury hadn't then added, "But it's odd, really. There are no mouse droppings – just strange trails of what looks like snail slime here and there. No slugs or snails, though. Maybe it's woodworm." She shook her head as Freddie froze.

Snail trails? *Wood*worm? Or, could it possibly be – surely not – *Book Worms*? In Portsteven Library? But how? They'd been keeping the Book Worms at bay back in Thesaurus. None had got close to the town itself, had they? He needed to speak to Meg right away. Book Worms couldn't be allowed to fester in the library. If they did, it would be an absolute disaster.

***

When Freddie filled Meg in on the situation at Portsteven Library, she agreed.

"This isn't good. I wonder how on earth they got there. Could they have been planted on you during the battle …?" She shook her head. "No, I don't think so. There was too much fighting going on – and Book Worms aren't that smart." Her face brightened, then dropped into a frown. "Hallow. *He's* that smart."

"The rogue Book-Keeper? But, how on earth could he have …? Ah, I see. While we were fighting?"

"That's my guess, anyway." Meg groaned. "The Book Worm attack must have been a ploy to empty the town so he could sneak in and deposit larvae in the library. I assume that's what we're dealing with at the moment, as they had to be small enough for Hallow to carry inside. But they'll grow quickly enough, especially in a library."

"Couldn't the Travelling Tree have prevented him?"

"I don't think it *can*," said Meg. "Although, what do any of us know about trees, really? They're as old as time itself and no doubt twice as wise. They're an enigma. If it *could* have stopped Hallow, it didn't and if that's the case, then there must be a reason."

"A good one, I hope," muttered Freddie.

"Trees only know 'good'," said Meg. "And if it *couldn't* stop him then there's no point in wondering about it. It happened, so now we need to deal with the consequences."

"How do we get rid of these Book Worms, then? Mum said she only saw the damage they've *started* doing – and what she thinks are snail trails."

"Fortunately for us, at this stage Book Worm larvae are much easier to dispose of than their parents," said Meg. "Which is why they're hiding. They're stupid but not *that* stupid. Nature has ways of knowing how to protect itself."

"OK then," said Freddie. "Let's get at it. Let's get these Book Worms out of Portsteven Library before they grow into an even bigger problem."

It was agreed that Meg would deal with the Book Worm larvae issue in Portsteven Library, as she could easily sneak in after closing time and leave out some special fodder for them.

"Once they eat these particular pages, which have been marinated in my potion, they'll lose all appetite for books and be rendered ordinary worms," she'd told Freddie proudly. "As long as they haven't grown too big already, I can then put them into a container and return them to our world as completely harmless creatures."

Unfortunately, Meg's antidote was only effective on baby Book Worms, but she was working on a secret alchemy project which aimed to create a mixture potent enough to make even a giant, adult Book Worm safe.

It was a work in progress.

In the meantime, she busied herself with soaking scrap pages in her special brew, carefully drying them out before packing them into her bag to take to Portsteven Library. When she arrived at the library she snuck out of her bookcase door and paused, listening for

Book Worm activity. The library was swaddled in silence but Meg's sharp hearing detected something which sounded like leaves dancing along a pavement.

The grubs were feeding.

Taking care not to disturb them, Meg went as close as she dared to the various shelves where she heard the Book Worm larvae feasting, leaving her own small pages for them to snack on. She tracked the noises all around the library, hopping from bookcase to bookcase, shelf to shelf, all through the night. She was exhausted by the end of it all, but satisfied with her efforts. She just hoped they paid off and that the larvae would eat *her* pages before the library opened, so she could collect them and return them to her own world. The marinade was designed to be irresistible to Book Worms, so it *should* work … At last, Meg returned to her doorway and sat down on the other side to wait.

As she leaned her head against the door, her eyes drooped and she yawned. There was no harm in taking a short nap before she checked the shelves again.

Meg closed her eyes and slept.

***

By the time the weary Book-Keeper awoke, a crack of light was shining into her hidey-hole. Meg rubbed her eyes, then jolted awake properly as she realised what had happened. It was morning – she'd slept right through the night and failed to collect the Book Worm larvae from the library.

She risked a peek out of the little door and heard voices – two women. They were coming closer so she ducked back inside and pulled the door towards her.

"Worms! Would you believe it?" said one of the voices. "They were eating the books and damaging the bookcases but now they're just sitting out in the open doing nothing. They're in almost every section!"

"Ugh, horrible little creatures," said the other voice. "At least we've spotted them before the public are allowed in. Can you imagine what people would say?"

"Yes and how it would affect the LAB's report on us," said the other voice, rich with worry. "It's not ideal that they're here, but for some reason they've stopped being pests and are now just sitting about looking unsightly …"

"And unsanitary."

"Yes, well, let's collect them and dispose of them and let that be the end of it. Honestly, every day these days there's some other problem to deal with!"

The talking ceased as the two women (one of whom must be Freddie's mum, Meg guessed) got to work. Meg grinned. Now that they were finishing off the job it was time for her to go.

***

By the time Saturday dawned, Freddie felt flooded by excitement and fear. What if Mr Tipett didn't go for coffee and a stroll today? What if they missed him? What if? What if? There were so many things which might go wrong. Everyone else was going to the Story Forest ahead of him, as they'd decided in the end that there would be too much activity in the bookshop if Meg was to transport all five of them at once. It was Freddie's job to lure Mr Tipett into the bookshop. All he could think was – what if I mess up? At least the Book Worm larvae problem in the library seemed to be cleared up. That was one less thing to worry about.

Before he left with Mercury to be dropped off at The

Painted Pot, where he'd told his mum he was meeting Brain, Rob and Gwen (only a half-lie, really), Freddie tucked the little fairy flute into his pocket. He intended to return it but also thought it might give him some leverage, should they run into any trouble in the forest. Surely a fairy flute had some magic that might prove itself useful?

He waved goodbye to his mum, then said hello to Penny in The Painted Pot, before ordering tea and a croissant and sitting down to wait for his quarry. He was early and hadn't been able to eat much at home, thanks to a stomach full of nerves. Penny smiled as she brought his order over, the croissant fresh and steaming from the oven.

"Where's the gang today then, Freddie?" she asked cheerily. "I hope my mother isn't imposing too much on you boys. She can be a handful!"

"No, she's great," said Freddie, picking a flake of golden pastry off the croissant. "We're, er, meeting soon, actually – down in the bookshop. I just thought I'd wait here instead of the library for a change. And mum doesn't like me eating down there," he added, hoping Penny wouldn't ask any more questions.

She smiled at him, then turned at the sound of more customers entering the café. "That's good. Well, I'll leave you to it, then. Enjoy."

Freddie *did* enjoy his extra breakfast and more than he expected to, considering. He was just swallowing his last mouthful of tea when Mr Tipett strode through the door. Freddie checked his watch. It was one minute to ten. He'd taken a seat tucked into the back corner of the tearoom but thanks to Gwen he knew that Mr Tipett always sat near the window, so the LAB inspector didn't even glance around for a seat, making a beeline instead for his usual spot. Freddie remained unseen.

Mr Tipett didn't loiter over his coffee and scone, which were delivered promptly to his table, as Freddie expected he demanded. He didn't strike Freddie as someone who was used to waiting for things. Freddie watched as his nemesis took quick bird-like sips of his coffee and rather huge bites of his scone, letting crumbs scatter all over the table and even onto the floor. He swiped more from his trousers onto the ground when he stood up to leave. He was like a particularly messy child. Mercury would never let her son make such a mess and Freddie added the behaviour to his steadily increasing mental list of 'crimes to the community' that Mr Tipett was guilty of.

Freddie felt like a spy as he slid from his own seat and tailed Mr Tipett out onto the promenade. His heart beat faster as they approached The Leaning Stack. It was a tall slim building squeezed in between two much fatter properties with wide windows – an art gallery and an electrical appliance shop.

Mr Tipett stopped to peer in at a picture in the gallery window and Freddie seized his chance before his quivering legs could take him in the other direction.

"Er, hello, Mr Tipett," he said, rather more loudly than he had intended. He fought back a blush as Mr Tipett turned to see who had spoken, his eyes widening and then quickly narrowing when he saw who it was.

"Good morning, young … Frederick, isn't it?"

"No, *Freddie*," said Freddie, through gritted teeth and a pasted-on smile. He knew Mr Tipett was well aware of his name and the council worker's replying smirk confirmed it.

"Of course. *Freddie*," he said. "Well, good morning to you, young man. I didn't think you'd want to talk to me, considering." Another smirk.

Freddie swallowed his anger but he felt hot. "Actually, I was wondering if I could show you something – in there." He pointed to The Leaning Stack.

Mr Tipett glanced at the bookshop and frowned. "Waste of good retail space, if you ask me," he said. "Why would I want to go in *there*?" He wrinkled his nose, as if Freddie had invited him into a foul-smelling swamp.

"Please," said Freddie. "It's important. And it might affect your decision with the library. In fact, I think it definitely will."

Mr Tipett studied the boy in front of him and Freddie tried to look as innocent as possible.

"I doubt it, boy. But, if I go in for two minutes, will you go away and leave me alone?"

"Yes, of course. Thanks Mr Tipett!" Relief washed over Freddie, as well as annoyance. Mr Tipett was really very rude. And as if Freddie would want to spend *any* time at all with the man who was trying to close down Portsteven Library and who hated everything to do with books.

"OK then. Lead on."

Mr Tipett looked as if he was stepping into a cesspit

rather than a book emporium whose shelves groaned under the weight of stories that Freddie now longed to explore. The council man actually held his nose as Freddie led him to a hidden corner at the back of the shop, which was thankfully empty at this time in the morning. He just hoped Meg had got the right bookcase.

Freddie tapped the shelf three times, making Mr Tipett jump.

"What on earth are you doing, boy?" he said in a nasally voice, fingers still pinching the bridge of his nose. "Now, what did you want to show me?"

For a moment Freddie panicked, then his heart leapt as he spied Meg's mischievous face poking out from behind a stack of books. The shelves were crammed with books piled horizontally and vertically; everywhere there was space there were books, so there were plenty of places for a Book-Keeper to hide. As Meg blew her coloured dust into Mr Tipett's surprised face, Freddie grinned.

"Just you wait and see, Mr Tipett!"

Chapter Twenty-seven

Tipett's Travels

The Story Forest tasted the metallic, synthetic and quite frankly, *sour* flavour of Mr Tipett as he unwittingly stumbled through the portal Meg had created in Portsteven and into the shady embrace of its many colossal trees. The Story Forest creaked in anticipation of what lay ahead. It did so enjoy a challenge and this was a particularly large one to stomach. A man who despised books had just breached its boundaries. Now *that* was going to require a bit of work.

The Book-Keeper girl had obviously brewed up an extra-special potion to bring them here directly. The Story Forest could taste the magic on them all, mingled in amongst their signature scents of self. The boy and

Book-Keeper were much more palatable than the man and the Story Forest could tell that there was more yet to be tasted from the boy. His flavour was still developing.

The Travelling Tree had already communicated as such.

Well, there was quite a group of them here now. The Story Forest would have to see that it did its work well before they departed.

***

Whatever alchemy Meg had used brought them not just to Book-Keeper territory but directly to the edge of the Story Forest itself. Of course, with the magical coloured powder also making them all Book-Keeper size, there was no discernible difference between Meg and Freddie so Mr Tipett had no reason to believe that she wasn't just a regular girl.

"It's best if he only remembers the forest, as he'll have to keep his memory of whatever happens here if this is going to work," whispered Meg.

"And will it?" asked Freddie, stepping swiftly aside

as Mr Tipett tried to grab him.

"We have to hope so!" said the Book-Keeper, dancing away from the bewildered Mr Tipett as he reached for her instead.

"What have you done? Where are we?" spluttered Mr Tipett. "This is … it's impossible! I was … I mean, we were … *You*!" He glared at Freddie. "You dragged me into that wretched fusty old *book*shop." He spat the last word as if it was poison. "Did you knock me out; is that what this is? One of your ridiculous library lovers probably helped you out, am I right? Knock our Mr Tipett and abandon him in a forest, eh, is *that* the plan?" He snorted, his face pale except for two deepening spots of red which had appeared high up on his jutting cheeks. "Well, it won't work, will it, because I'm awake now and I'll be reporting this incident – you can count on that, young man. And young lady."

He turned his glare on Meg. "You can't just ambush a local government employee and expect to get away with it! And let me tell you this – it certainly won't help your cause any. In fact," Mr Tipett pointed to each of them in turn, a triumphant sneer spreading across his face, "I daresay it will be the final nail in the coffin for

Portsteven Library. Ha! Thanks for assisting *my* cause!"

Freddie knew Mr Tipett was just taunting them but he couldn't help feeling worried by his words. He glanced at Meg, who shrugged.

"This is the way out," she told Mr Tipett. "You've got to go through the forest to get back to where you were."

Mr Tipett peered into the Story Forest's gloom. "I am *not* going in there! I demand you take me back properly. Whoever helped you kidnap me must have a car of some sort." He looked around as if expecting one to be parked nearby. "I don't quite remember how I got here, but there *must* be a car," he muttered.

"Er, not quite," said Freddie.

"Look," said Meg. "We're not scared of you, so don't threaten us. You can either follow us into the forest or you can stay here and find your own way home. Come on, Freddie, let's go." She pulled Freddie towards the trees. Freddie wasn't sure he'd have the courage to speak to an adult like that, even Mr Tipett, but he was impressed that Meg had.

"Don't worry. He's bound to follow," she whispered. "He's too afraid not to."

And sure enough, when Freddie sneaked a glance

behind him a few minutes later he saw Mr Tipett trailing them with a sullen look on his face.

***

It wasn't long before Freddie and Meg caught sight of Brain, Rob and Gwen, who were waiting for them a little way ahead, not far from where they'd entered the Story Forest. Mr Tipett was keeping himself deliberately at a distance so they had time for a quick debrief before he caught up.

"I think it's best if we split up," said Meg. "This is something Mr Tipett has to experience for himself, *by* himself. We can lead him in but he has to find his own story."

"What if he doesn't play ball?" said Rob.

"Oh, the Story Forest won't allow that," said Meg with a smile. "It makes certain demands of all who travel through it, so he'll have to interact with it whether he wants to or not."

"I would love to see what happens to him," said Gwen. "But, no matter! We're here, boys, so let's go and see what this wonderful Story Forest has to show *us*! If you need us, just yodel!"

Meg raised her eyebrows as the Silver Surfer shuffled off into the trees. Brain and Rob shrugged, then grinned and followed her. "Don't worry," said Rob over his shoulder. "We remember how to summon you."

"Will they be OK?" asked Freddie.

"They should be fine. I gave them a simple spell so they can summon me if they encounter any major trouble. And we've agreed to meet back at the edge of the forest later. The Story Forest isn't really *that* dangerous, well, unless you run into Book Worms … But I'm sure they'll enjoy it!"

"Who was that?" demanded Mr Tipett as he finally caught up with them. "More library hooligans, eh? Run off instead of facing the music? Mark my word, there will be consequences!"

Meg and Freddie said nothing as they began walking again. The trees were growing much closer together now, their branches whispering in the gloom. It was cool and smelt of fresh pine. For a while they heard Mr Tipett trudging behind them, muttering complaints. His sounds were absorbed into the forest the further in they went, blending with the rest of the scurryings and toings and fro-ings around them until they couldn't distinguish one sound from the next.

It was a subtle change in the atmosphere a short time later that made them both stop.

Something was missing amongst the general hubbub of the forest. Meg and Freddie turned to check on Mr Tipett, but he was gone.

***

No one ever found out exactly what happened to Mr Tipett in the Story Forest that day, at the heart of nature's very own living library of words, where letters sprouted from the trees and pages ate them glutinously if offered (and also if not).

Here, red herrings lay in wait for unsuspecting souls, luring them in with false hopes and unsatisfying conclusions, while stony bridges proffered more reliable story arcs over story streams, and dreams floated like baubles in the air.

In the Story Forest, fairies danced and sang and led travellers to forbidden feasts and rainbow waterfalls behind whose cascading curtains lay hidden treasures hoarded by even more well-concealed creatures.

Did Mr Tipett find magic or mayhem – or both – during his time in the Story Forest? Was he still a villain or did he emerge as the hero of his story, a role he seemed to have cast himself in already, despite public disagreement? Did his plot twist and turn like the river charging through the forest; did he find a sidekick or a nemesis along the way?

Did stories come alive for Mr Tipett in the Story Forest, words working wizardry on his unimaginative mind and opening up new worlds of possibility to him? Did he feast on the lifeblood of this sacred place and allow it to change him from within?

It is a secret the Story Forest keeps.

It is a story only Mr Tipett can tell ...

Chapter Twenty-eight

An Unexpected Invitation

One minute Mr Tipett was, begrudgingly, following those two annoying children – the librarian's red-headed son had found himself a strange female friend who had seemingly helped trick him to wherever *this* was – the next moment, all he could see were trees. It was as if the two of them had vanished into thin air, which was impossible, of course.

Mr Tipett shouted that they'd better come out from wherever they were hiding, right this minute, because he just knew they were toying with him – and he wouldn't have it. First, they'd kidnapped him and brought him to the middle of nowhere (he still hadn't quite worked out *how*, but they surely had); now they'd left him stranded while they no doubt had a laugh at his expense in their secret hiding place.

Timothy Tipett very much disliked books. Now, he'd developed a distinct dislike of children too. He'd never really given them much thought since he'd stopped *being* one of them but it appeared that they were just another nuisance he needed to contain and control.

"Just like your father did to you ..."

Mr Tipett jumped. It sounded as if the voice was in his head, but that wasn't *his* thought. It wasn't *his* voice. Someone else had invaded his mind.

He shook his head. Nonsense. He was just letting himself get spooked by this strange old forest. There was no one in his head but himself and he certainly wasn't going to let those *kids* see him get rattled.

Mr Tipett straightened his back, fixed his tie and walked on.

***

The Story Forest closed in around Mr Tipett like an unwelcome hug as he strayed further into its depths, seeing only what he wanted to see – initially. Mr Tipett had no interest in trees, so he failed to cast his eyes upwards, where boughs grew waxy letters, the raw ingredients for crafting stories dangling mere inches from his face. He didn't look at the gnarled trunks, fissured with life and with secret doors carved into their timber. He dismissed the sparks swirling ahead as "dratted insects" when really, if he'd taken a closer look, he'd have found himself in the presence of fairies. His mind was closed to the possibility of 'other' and 'imagination'; he had no desire to interact with his surroundings other than to get very quickly through and away from them.

Mr Tipett only looked for things he thought might be useful to himself, so when he finally spotted a figure up ahead, he smiled with satisfaction and made a beeline towards it. The figure had its back to Mr Tipett and appeared to be busy defacing the trees, drawing or writing on one of them as Mr Tippet approached. It seemed odd sort of behaviour but then, how on earth was *he* supposed to know what people got up to in forests? Give him his clean fourth-floor office any day, with its polished floor and tidy desk, over this dark and, quite frankly – yes, he would admit it – *creepy* old forest.

Mr Tipett hesitated, doubting now whether he should actually approach this person after all. He could be anyone. A vagabond! A criminal! He could be a murderer taking refuge in here from the authorities and now here he, Mr Tipett, was about to walk right up to him and ask for his help. What if he was attacked? (It seemed there was a spark of imagination in Mr Tipett after all, thought the Story Forest). Granted, it did look as if the person was scribbling on trees (an eccentric artist, perhaps?), but that didn't really instil Mr Tipett with calm. Indeed, it quite unnerved him, actually. A loopy creative person was just as unwelcome to him at this (and any other) moment as a murderer was.

Such was the way that Mr Tipett's mind worked. All of this flashed through his head like lightning. Unfortunately, the final step he took before stopping in his tracks to reconsider his options saw his foot land quite heavily upon some scattered twigs and the very distinct cracking of them under his weight made the figure spin round.

Mr Tipett took an automatic step backwards as he felt himself almost physically shrinking under the dark glare of his potential saviour, or tormentor's, narrowed eyes. It was a man – wiry with muscle and about as tall as Mr Tipett. He was dressed all in black but appeared immaculately kitted out (Mr Tipett always noted cleanliness and a tidy appearance), which automatically made Mr Tipett trust him a little more, despite the glare. His eyes were a startling rich green – Mr Tipett might have likened their colour to moss if his mind worked in that way. It didn't, so he thought of emeralds instead. He smiled at the man and extended his arm.

"Hello. My name's Tipett – Timothy Tipett. Sorry to, er, startle you, sir, but I seem to be lost and wondered if I could ask you for some directions?"

The man in black frowned, then reassembled his features into a neutral expression. It was certainly a much less aggressive one, which soothed Mr Tipett somewhat.

"You're not from around here?"

"Er, no. Well, I don't think so. I mean, I don't actually know where I am, but I'm not familiar with this …" Mr Tipett glanced around him, at a loss.

"Forest?" supplied the man, his eyes conveying something that could either be amusement or danger. Mr Tipett really wasn't sure.

"Yes. This forest. I was brought here against my will, you see. I must have been knocked out. I mean, one minute I was in that musty old second-hand bookshop, where that dratted *boy* took me, the next, I'm here in this place with the boy and an annoying girl, who I can only assume helped him in bringing me here. For whatever reason. Well, I mean, for the reason of threatening me, or getting rid of me – that's what *I* think. They're probably deluded enough to believe that if I'm out of the way their precious library will be saved. Well, it won't!"

The stranger listened to all of this with rapt attention and Mr Tipett hoped he wasn't coming across as a madman. It *did* sound a bit bizarre when he put it all together like that. As he talked, however, the stranger seemed to become more and more interested and he even gave a wispy smile at the end of Mr Tipett's rant.

"I think you and I might be able to assist one another, Mr Tipett. It sounds as though we have a shared dislike of libraries and I assume, therefore, of books also?"

Mr Tipett nodded.

"Excellent. I think I know the children you speak of. Troublesome pair, by all accounts, but we needn't worry about them right now. Perhaps you could help me with something and in return I'll help *you* back to wherever it is you'd prefer to be. I think we share a joint interest, Mr Tipett, I really do."

"Perfect," said Mr Tipett. "And what do you need help with, Mr, ah ..?"

"Hallow. You can call me Hallow."

***

Mr Tipett thought Hallow a little, well, *odd*, but they had sort of bonded over a shared dislike of books, libraries and children – the redhead and curly-haired girl in particular – so Mr Tipett had agreed to help him in any way he could, provided he got home safely and as quickly as possible. He had a library inspection to complete and a report to write, after all. Hallow agreed that it was important he completed that very pertinent work, which made Mr Tipett smile with pleasure. It was nice to have someone appreciate him for a change.

When he asked Hallow what exactly he wanted help with, however, he didn't feel quite as cheerful.

"We're going to set the forest on fire," said Hallow,

mossy eyes glinting.

Mr Tipett was aghast. He wouldn't exactly call himself a lover of forests, particularly this one, but surely that was a bit extreme? Also, he was a respected councillor and Library Administration Body board member. He couldn't become an arsonist. That would make him a criminal! He visibly paled.

"Why do you need my help with that?" he asked.

"Well, as you may have noticed, this is no ordinary forest, so setting it alight takes a little more ... effort, you could say."

Mr Tipett hadn't noticed anything of the sort but as he looked around at the trees he suddenly realised there *was* something a bit unusual about them. "Are those," he squinted up at the branches nearest him, "*letters*?" His mouth dropped open.

"Do you really not know what this place is?"

"Of course not! I told you – I'm lost!"

"Yes, you said. I just didn't realise ... Well, anyway, this is the Story Forest and we're going to burn it down. Think of it as the ultimate library – the original teller of tales; the supermarket for authors and readers and those with," Hallow spat the word, "*imaginations*."

Mr Tipett stared at the rogue Book-Keeper. "And why does it need two of us to destroy it? Don't leaf *letters* burn just as easily as ordinary leaves?"

"*Because,* Mr Tipett, the forest is magic, and magic needs magic to destroy it. Your run-of-the-mill fire won't work on the Story Forest. And two people will make that job a whole lot quicker and easier."

Mr Tipett was still trying to wrap his mind around the sentence which had the word 'magic' in it three times. It wasn't a word he allowed in his vocabulary and now there it was, thrice! He wasn't about to get mixed up in whatever voodoo this Hallow was involved with – and turn himself into an arsonist, hunted by the police. Mr Tipett may want to eradicate books and libraries, but he was perfectly capable of fulfilling his objectives within the parameters of the law. How on earth was he going to give Hallow the slip, though? He looked as if he would be able to keep Mr Tipett here by force, if needs be, with that steely frame of his.

"*Try the door,*" a voice whispered.

Someone was in his head – again! There was no doubt about it this time. Mr Tipett had had enough. He needed to escape from this creepy forest, this menacing man and this downright *rude* voice which kept trespassing into his thoughts. And what *door*, anyway? All he could see were trees! He looked around.

Ah, trees with the outlines of doors on their trunks. Why should he be surprised at that? This place was beyond anything he'd ever thought a forest was like.

"Well?" said Hallow, impatience flaring behind his eyes.

"I, er ... Let me just think for a moment."

Mr Tipett didn't have a clue what he was doing as he strode over to a tree with a tall, thin rectangular door gouged into its trunk. This was ludicrous. Ridiculous. Impossible and silly. He would look preposterous when it didn't work and then Hallow would know what he'd been planning and then he'd really be in for it.

But as Mr Tipett approached the tree, the strangest thing yet happened. A golden light began to outline the door and he saw it open a crack. As he pushed against it and stepped over the threshold he heard Hallow bellow out, "*No!*" just before Mr Tipett was swallowed up by the tree.

The door clicked shut and disappeared.

Chapter Twenty-nine
Tipett's Transformation

Trees have their own secrets and each works in its own special way – particularly in the Story Forest – but, of course, Mr Tipett had no idea what to expect when he stepped through that woody door. He lacked the imagination to think beyond entry to the tree, so the idea of entering a portal into another world – another time or place – never occurred to him. At most, he considered in those fleeting moments that it might make a good hiding place. He certainly didn't entertain any thoughts towards what *actually* happened, which was that the tree truly did swallow Mr Tipett.

Mr Tipett became the tree.

It happened like this.

Once Mr Tipett was inside the trunk and the door clicked shut, darkness coddled him, followed swiftly by showers of golden sparks raining down around him. For a snippet of a second he reconsidered his decision of entering the colossal trunk and reached for where the door had been. It was of course now, alas, no more. All was in darkness and Mr Tipett had a strange sensation of his body being there but also, not quite there. It felt light and airy, like a jumble of particles rather than solid flesh and bone. What was happening to him? And yet, he felt weirdly calm and didn't try to resist whatever was occurring. Part of him sensed it would be futile, anyway.

His limbs lightened, arms slowly extending upwards and outwards, his legs growing down into the ground, stretching to impossible lengths, yet causing Mr Tipett no pain at all. It made him a little giddy and he really thought he ought to be panicking at this bizarre metamorphosis that he seemed to be undergoing but then, it couldn't *really* be happening – could it? He was hallucinating, surely.

And yet.

Mr Tipett felt safe and more alive than he'd ever felt

before. The growing process speeded up, suddenly, and he felt himself becoming something entirely different from what he had been mere minutes (or perhaps hours?) before. Here, he had no concept of time and how quickly or slowly it passed. As Mr Tipett's limbs settled into their new shapes, he was filled with the most wondrous feeling. It was as if he'd just crested a mountain and seen stunning landscapes spread out in all their glory beneath him; as if he'd slept for a hundred years and then re-awoken with only zesty enthusiasm in his veins. It was as if he'd been granted every wish he'd ever had – and more besides.

That's how wonderful Mr Tipett now felt.

He felt 90 feet tall, which in fact, he was, now being an impressive oak tree of considerable – but not yet full – vintage in the Story Forest.

Mr Tipett wriggled his fingers and his branches played piano in the air. He wriggled his toes and his roots shifted in the soil. He tilted his head and the topmost part of his oaken-self bowed slightly. He smelt rain in the far north and heard whispers on the breeze. In his roots he understood many important things about survival – both his and that of the forest and the creatures who lived within it. And, of course, with his lettery leaves, he tasted the infinite potential of stories. They sang to him as clearly as birdsong, though no one but the trees could hear such music. Inspiration and imagination flowed through Mr Tipett's arboreal veins, fuelled by life rich with opportunity – and all of this made Mr Tipett think.

He thought about letters and words and how they jig-sawed into sentences, which could be enlightening and exciting and beautiful – something Mr Tipett hadn't really considered before. He'd become the oak and, as such, had become part of the Story Forest, interconnected as it was by the extensive root system of its many trees. He now had the ability to hear and understand their underground communications, as well as those messages carried across the air. The trees had tales to tell and for once, Mr Tipett was inclined to listen.

Perhaps the Story Forest had planned it like this all along. For Mr Tipett to fully understand and truly appreciate the power and significance of stories, maybe he had to become tree. Or, perhaps there were other ways the Story Forest could have made his time within its boundaries count and this was merely one of them –

the specific path which had drawn Mr Tipett towards it, despite the others that lay open to him. Whatever the answer, this was the way in which Mr Tipett's tale had unfolded and he relaxed into it in a way most unbecoming of him.

The literary lifeblood he had, up until now, lacked was saturating his system and he'd never felt better.

He was amazed. Astounded. He was absolutely bowled over by what he was experiencing. Did other people know about this, he wondered? Did that librarian's boy with his shock of red hair know how powerful stories were? Did his mother understand the joy and the heart-fluttering moments a story could induce in a person? And, if stories could do all that and more, then books – those papery gems which gave stories their physical bodies – were precious. And there he, Mr Tipett, was trying to shut down his local library and had taken such pleasure in eradicating bookshops and anything book-related throughout his adult life.

He was appalled. Embarrassed and downright ashamed. How many people had he deprived of stories over the years? It appeared that the bitter tang of regret had now entered Mr Tipett's veins.

And so, the Story Forest continued its work. No one was truly a lost cause before they had the opportunity to reconsider their ways and it seemed as though Mr Tipett was doing just that. He soaked up the stories he'd missed out on as a boy, caught wind of tales in the air that flowed like silk through his branches. He absorbed more enlightenment from the soil and listened carefully to the knowledge his roots conveyed. Mr Tipett found that he couldn't get enough, but no one should ever have too much of a good thing – and certainly not too much of a wonderfully magnificent thing – so the Story Forest allowed him only so much precious time as an oak and before very long, it was time for the former book-hating councillor to return to his own form and leave the forest behind.

Of course, Mr Tipett's own mind was much too small and human-shaped to retain all of what he had experienced, but it held onto enough memories and feelings to ensure that when he emerged from the Story Forest, he had a sparkle in his eyes and a changed disposition.

Mr Tipett had been transformed.

***

Freddie and Meg, meanwhile, had somehow found themselves back in the fairy glade – almost as if the Story Forest was guiding them there, which, of course, it was.

"Oh Freddie, you didn't!" said Meg crossly.

"I wanted to return it," said Freddie, pulling the fairy flute from his pocket. "I couldn't just leave it there that time; it would have been destroyed by the Book Worms."

"The fairies won't necessarily see it that way, Freddie."

Indeed, the fairies started chattering as soon as they spotted the two children and the flute's owner sped straight over to Freddie, gesticulating wildly at him.

"Alright, alright," he said. "As I was just explaining to *Meg*, I only took the flute to keep it safe. If I'd stolen it, why would I have brought it back with me and not hidden it at home?"

The fairies' protestations quietened a little and the flute owner also calmed down once Freddie solemnly presented the instrument on his open palm. The fairy seized it with delight, then darted away to inspect it. Freddie and Meg watched the little creature closely, waiting to see what it would do next. The fairies were all quite androgynous in their appearance, so Freddie wasn't sure if it was a male or female fairy whom he might have offended or, perhaps, made friends with.

He was still trying to decide which it was when the fairy fixed him with a quizzical look before appearing to reach a decision about something. It seemed satisfied with the condition of the flute and put it away safely in its pocket, then cupped its hands and started chanting. Something shimmered and sparkled in front of the creature and, quick as lightning, the fairy plucked it from the air. Before Freddie could blink, the fairy had darted back over to him and dropped something over his head. He felt a coolness fall against his neck and that was how Freddie found himself the recipient of a very special gift indeed.

A fairy wish.

Chapter Thirty

Alchemy

Brain, Rob and Gwen were waiting for them at the edge of the Story Forest when Freddie and Meg returned from the fairy glade.

"Where's Tipett?" said Rob. "And what's that around your neck, Fred?" He pointed at a silver chain adorned with a single glittering gem, shaped like a teardrop.

"We led Tipett as far into the forest as we could and then it took him on his way," said Meg. "Oh, and that's a fairy wish Freddie has." She grinned.

"A wish? From a *fairy*?" Gwen's face filled with sunshine. "How marvellous! However did you manage that, young man?"

"Surely that's everything solved then?" said Brain.

"If you have a wish, Fred, you can just wish that Tipett doesn't close the library."

"I don't think it's that simple," said Freddie, glancing at Meg.

"It's not," said the Book-Keeper. "You could wish that Tipett doesn't close the library but that just means someone *else* might do it instead. You have to be very specific with fairy wishes and anyway, they shouldn't be used to change people's intentions. You should *never* meddle with minds. Fairies like to cause mischief so although it *is* a gift to be granted a fairy wish, you must be *very* careful how you use it.

"To protect the library for the future we need more than a wish. We need a community prepared to fight for it – people who will love it and use it regularly – and a local government that will help them maintain it. I think we have the first; let's just hope the Story Forest has helped with the second."

"I wonder what adventures Mr Tipett has been having in there," said Gwen, peering into the trees. "I do hope it has changed him for the better! I must say, *we* had a wonderful time, didn't we boys?" She winked at Brain and Rob. "We'll tell you and Meg all about it later."

"Yeah, so what now?" interrupted Rob. "Do we all just wait here and hope he reappears? Might be ages."

"Let's hope he hasn't been eaten by a Book Worm," said Brain. "Actually ..."

"Let's hope he *has*?" said Rob, raising his eyebrows quizzically.

Brain blushed. "No, I didn't mean —"

"It's OK, Brain. I'll just remember never to get on your bad side, in case you feed me to the Book Worms."

"Now, boys," chided Gwen. "Don't say such things." She looked into the forest again. "All the same, I don't like the idea of meeting those Book Worms. Perhaps we should all go home and wait for Mr Tipett there in, er, safety?"

"Me and Meg will wait here for him," said Freddie. "Meg, can you send everyone else back?"

She nodded. "Yes, I think the fewer of us waiting for Mr Tipett the better. I can send you all back now, if we're agreed?" Brain and Rob looked a little disappointed but they nodded all the same, so Meg took out her coloured powder and Freddie watched as his friends faded from view like a memory.

"That stuff's brilliant," he said.

"Yes, it's a lot more potent than the powder I usually use on you," said Meg. "It's much more effective at transporting people directly from place to place. It resizes the subject *and* takes them to their destination. Two jobs in one."

"I wish I knew how to make potions," said Freddie. "It would definitely make school a lot more interesting if we were taught how to do magic."

"Being an apprentice alchemist is hard work, but it has its uses all right," said Meg. "I can't pass on any trade secrets, though – sorry."

"I thought you might say that!" Freddie glanced into the trees. "Do you think we should look for Mr Tipett? I mean, *he* won't know to come back here, will he?"

"Oh, the Story Forest will bring him back out eventually," said Meg knowingly. "You'll see."

They waited and waited and finally, as the shadows around them lengthened and contorted into all kinds of strange shapes, Freddie heard footsteps and a voice floating through the trees. He strained his ears. Was that the sound of a happy voice or an angry one? Could the Story Forest *really* have worked its magic in such a way as to transform Mr Tipett?

The LAB inspector's lanky frame strode out of the forest and headed straight for them. Mr Tipett's mouth was pressed tightly together and his face wore a frown. Freddie's heart sank.

"You!" Mr Tipett pointed at Meg. "I demand that you take me home, immediately!"

***

When they reappeared in the second-hand bookshop Freddie expected it to be much later than it was. They'd been gone for some hours but he was glad to see that the shop was still open and that there would be no explaining to do with Mercury. He'd told his mum he'd be with his friends all day, so she wouldn't be looking for him. Yet.

Mr Tipett stared at each of them in turn before spinning on his heel and striding out of the bookshop and along the prom. Meg and Freddie looked at one another.

"Don't worry, Freddie. He's had a very unusual day and we don't know what he experienced in the Story

Forest. All may not be lost. We'll just have to wait and see."

"Thanks, Meg." Freddie hoped she was right. *Had* Tippett been transformed? Could the Story Forest have shown him the magic of a good story and won him over with words? He wasn't sure, but if the Story Forest couldn't do it then there was no hope for the rest of them.

He was just trying to work out if the spark he'd seen in Mr Tipett's eyes when he fixed Freddie with that stare was due to a change of heart, or a deepening of hatred.

***

Hallow also had Mr Tipett on his mind, as he was keen to know what had happened to the human after he stepped into the oak tree. Especially as he'd never reappeared again. Hallow had waited.

He could only wait for so long, however, as he had other things to do, but still, he was curious. He knew others came and went through the trunks but he'd never been permitted to himself and he thought it very unlikely that he ever would be. Just what was the Story

Forest up to? Well, he still intended to burn it down, whether he had the human's help or not. He was Hallow, after all, and he was more than capable. An extra pair of hands would have been handy, though.

The Story Forest was protected by ancient magic – perhaps as old as the world itself – but Hallow had filled his time with plenty of research, tracking down other isolated and bitter Book-Keepers (though they rejected the name) and gleaning nuggets of very useful information along the way.

Like the fact that the Story Forest could only burn when its timber was painted with a rare elixir composed of very special ingredients and brewed in a very unique fashion. First of all, various precious oils sourced from every corner of the planet had to be carefully blended together, with a timeworn spell chanted over the concoction as it simmered under a fat, full moon. Even better with two moons. The vessel which bore such a toxic potion also had to be one forged from silver and sap – ideally sap from the Story Forest itself, as this was more potent, though any would suffice.

Hallow had hunted down all of these elements; he'd made the potion and vessel, pieced together the spell and done everything in accordance with what he'd been told by numerous devious characters across the years. Now, at last, this was his big moment and no one was here to stop him. Granted, no one was around to *help* him either – that Mr Tipett had seemed like a godsend until he'd disappeared – but Hallow was himself forged from grit and determination and one pair of hands would just have to do, as it had been planned previously. Well, there was no better 'Book-Keeper' for the job.

Hallow had chosen this clearing specially, as it was drenched in moonlight that didn't penetrate the forest elsewhere, and he had painted each of the trunks around its perimeter with his lethal brew. Once these infected trees were alight, the enchanted fire would quickly engulf the rest of the forest. He sighed in anticipation of a job pretty much well done. His arms ached and his back was a bit stiff and creaky from all of his work but he felt for the first time in forever as if he'd really accomplished something. When the Story Forest burned, his soul – or whatever he had in place of one – would be soothed. He felt almost giddy but attributed that to the sulphurous fumes wafting up from his potion. The timber had soaked it up readily and Hallow was greedy for the next part of his plan.

The striking of the match.

Or, rather, the striking of a very particular type of flint found in the depths of a lonely cave inhabited by a dragon, struck against another flint from an opposing dragon cavern, which would then light a long phoenix feather. This, in turn, would ignite the oily trees. Really, it was a spell-and-a-half, this one, but it took a lot to beat the Story Forest and beat it he would.

Hallow struck the flints.

Sparks flew and he lit the phoenix feather.

The feather became swollen with rainbow fire and Hallow laid it against the first trunk, flames licking the wood.

***

The rest of the weekend passed without any further adventures for Freddie and his friends and was filled instead with homework and household chores. Freddie threw himself into it all gladly, welcoming the distraction.

On Monday, meanwhile, Brain and Rob filled his head with their tales from the Story Forest, which involved a grumpy goblin, being chased through a cavern of gold and grappling with some argumentative plants. They'd loved every minute of it.

At home, all was as it had been, though Mercury still sang less around the house and didn't mention the library. They had done what they could. All they were able to do now was wait.

"Show must go on, Fred," said Mercury with a sigh.

The envelope, when it arrived on a rather grey Saturday morning, was large and brown and delivered not to the library, but to Mercury May's home.

It was from the LAB.

Chapter Thirty-one

The Miracle

Freddie had never known the atmosphere in his home to be so tense. His mother carried the envelope reverently into the kitchen, placed it on the table and then stood back from it, as if she was afraid it was going to jump up and bite her.

"Do you want me to open it, mum?" asked Freddie.

"No, thanks Fred, but I think I'd better do this myself." She sighed. "Best to treat it like a plaster – rip it off quickly," she muttered. "It's come earlier than I was expecting. I don't know what *that* means ..."

She hesitated, then grabbed the envelope and tore it open, pulling out the pages from within, scanning them furtively. Freddie watched as his mother's eyes slowly widened, then narrowed, a frown furrowing Mercury's brow. He felt his hope flicker, then die.

"I don't … I don't understand," said Mercury. "But I don't have to!" She gave a loud whoop, jolting Freddie out of his body and back again. "We're saved, Fred! We've done it. We've *actually* done it! Mr Tipett – the Library Administration Body – is keeping the library open. He's written a *glowing* report! And what's more, they're going to do a multi-million pound renovation. Can you believe it?!"

Her eyes were diamonds and her smile was a rainbow and all Freddie could say was, "Brilliant."

***

In the meantime, the Story Forest burned.

***

The good news about the library spread like a charm across Portsteven and Freddie's father, of course, made it a front-page story in the newspaper the following Monday. The headline announced:

Portsteven Library saved!

LAB pledges £2m investment to revamp treasured community resource

At school, Ms Woods congratulated the boys on doing their bit for the library with the radio interview and peaceful protest, along with the other pupils who had shown their support.

"You see, class," she said, beaming. "It just goes to show what can happen when a community gets together and uses its voice for good! All we had to do, in the end, was make it clear just how much we love – and need – our library."

Brain, Rob and Freddie shared a look. They knew that in this case it had taken a little more work with Mr Tipett, but it had certainly been a team effort and the library would have been a goner if they hadn't done something about it.

They met Gwen, who was at the library with Graham and the rest of the Silver Surfers, after school on Monday. Freddie had rung her immediately on Saturday, of course, to share the news. She waved a copy of his dad's newspaper as he came into the library with his friends.

"A job well done, boys! A job *very* well done," she said, giving them an exaggerated wink. "It seems our Mr Tipett has undergone quite a change of heart! If you see your little friend again, do pass on my profound thanks, will you?"

"Of course," said Freddie. He didn't say much as they celebrated, his mum having laid on a mini tea party in the library that day for everyone. For once, it wasn't a place of comfortable silence and tranquillity but of course today, nobody minded.

The thing was, Freddie hadn't seen Meg since they'd returned from the Story Forest with Mr Tipett and he was worried that something was up.

***

In Thesaurus, the Travelling Tree began to smoke – plumes of rainbow breath drifting down from its lofty branches …

***

Hallow couldn't believe it.

The Story Forest was alight.

For once, he'd done something right – or something *wrong*, depending on which perspective you viewed his little spot of enchanted arson from.

He watched from a safe distance, perched atop a hunchbacked mountain, legs dangling over the precipice. It felt odd, now the initial elation had passed. Destroying the Story Forest had been a part of his life's mission for so long – it had fuelled his desire, if such a word could be applied to someone who had never felt passionate about anything, really. Not even her – *them*. He was certain of that. Pretty much, almost one hundred percent, absolutely certain ...

Anyway, the Story Forest had been his silent, brooding nemesis for so long that he almost felt saddened to see it go, albeit in a glorious blaze of multi-coloured smoke. He needed a new life goal now, but what? There was still some minor work to be done with polluting libraries and destroying books but he needed something Story Forest-worthy to fill this unexpected void that had just cracked open inside him.

It was a predicament.

Hallow waited while the forest burned. However, it covered a vast area and the flames showed no sign of abating any time soon, so eventually, he nodded off. He awoke hours later within a haze of lettered air.

Words danced around him, giddy with colour, shining slickly in the pale sun. Or moon? Hallow had no idea how long he'd been asleep. Anyway, this didn't seem right. He swiped at the letters, some of them clustering into words just beyond his reach and he squinted to read them, despite himself.

He frowned.

"*Thank* you?" he muttered. "For what? And from whom?"

A creeping dread filled his stomach as more words formed in the smoky air and he read on.

'*Regards, from the Story Forest.*

You fed us precious oils from the ends of the earth.

You mixed them with care and spoke an age-old spell.

You simmered the elixir under a fat, full moon, poured it into a sacred silver vessel then painted us with a phoenix feather aflame with dragon-flint fire.'

The letters spun wildly in the air as they raced to

form new words, fresh sentences.

'The Story Forest has never been stronger. Thank you.'

Hallow read the airy transcript in disbelief, yet a strange mellowness tip-toed through him the more he read. Relief? No, definitely not. Only in so much as it reinstated his life goal – to destroy the wretched place. So, the Story Forest had tricked him, had it? Well, he could try again.

As Hallow digested the final words hovering above him, they dissolved into nothing, a few fizzling out like sparklers. The smoke disappeared with them and the rogue Book-Keeper cast his eyes downwards. The Story Forest was a sea of lush green and sparkling rainbows. The tips of its trees seemed to bow in acknowledgement to him and he felt – he felt … what? Pleased? Satisfied? Happy at someone, albeit the enemy, appreciating his misguided efforts?

Something bubbled deep inside Hallow.

He tried to quell it.

It only bubbled more ferociously.

Hallow couldn't help it. What could he do? The Story Forest had bettered him, played him at his own game.

He did something now that he couldn't remember

ever doing before.

Hallow laughed.

Chapter Thirty-two

Revelations

I
t was as if she sensed his desperation, for that night, Meg appeared. Freddie breathed a sigh of relief.

"I thought, I thought you'd, well —"

"Gone? Not yet. But I *will* go, Fred, sorry. It's just the way it is. We Book-Keepers only appear to humans in times of great need and it seems that *your* time of need is now over. We did it – we saved the library. Anyway, I've actually been a bit busy since we last spoke because – and you'll never believe this – someone tried to *burn down* the Story Forest! I mean, it didn't work, obviously," she said, as Freddie's eyes became saucers. "The old Story Forest is cleverer than that. I don't think anything *can* kill it, or if it can, it's a secret hidden so deep that no one living will ever find it. We think it's

Hallow who was behind the attempt but, of course, *he's* disappeared. Good riddance, I say. Although, we probably haven't heard the last from him."

"What about the Book Worms?" asked Freddie.

"Well, now that Portsteven Library's clearly protected and is showing signs of getting even stronger, the Book Worms have backed off," said Meg. "And Hallow hasn't tried anything else, so I think we've really done it, Freddie!"

"Well, I wouldn't have done anything if you hadn't got me involved," said Freddie. He sighed. "Do you really have to go, though?"

"We're a secretive people, Fred. How many Book-Keepers have you encountered – spoken to – since all this began? No one, really, apart from me. Well, there was the Book Worm battle and you met my mum, briefly, but it's rare that humans experience so much contact with us. We keep to ourselves, Freddie. That's just the way it is. Besides, now you have a newfound love of stories, you'll have those to keep you busy instead."

"Can't I have both?"

Meg laughed. "You've had more than most, Freddie,

so, no. Can you say goodbye to Brain, Rob, Gwen and Graham for me?"

He nodded.

"Don't worry. Gwen saw another Book-Keeper as an adult, so you never know when you might see me – or some other Book-Keeper – again. But you *will* see me, Freddie. I'm sure of it." She winked.

"Gwen's ancient, though!" he protested. "I can't wait that long. I don't even know if I'll *live* that long!"

"You'll be too busy growing up to miss me, I promise," said Meg. "But we'll always be back there, on the other side of the bookcases, be they metal or wood or anything else. While there's books on shelves, the Book-Keepers will be around. Now, I have a present for you."

She pulled a package out of the little door she'd made in Freddie's bookcase, blew some of her coloured powder onto it and then handed it to Freddie. It grew to fill his palm and he found himself holding a book.

"I said I'd find you something that would help make you develop a love of reading, didn't I?" The Book-Keeper grinned. "Well, you love reading now anyway, but this will make you never want to stop. See you around, Fred."

"Thanks Meg. I'll see you around," said Freddie as Meg gave him a final grin before stepping into the bookcase, the door closing with a click behind her.

***

Meg didn't do goodbyes. In fact, she hated them, so she'd made sure she didn't drag it out with Freddie. It was better that way. Rules were rules with the Book-Keepers so there was no point in getting too attached to humans unless she wanted to get into serious trouble. Book-Keepers could be banished for fraternising with humans outside of a crisis which demanded they work together and, as she'd just told Freddie, their current crisis was now over.

Besides, as much as she enjoyed spending time with Freddie, Meg was a bit distracted right now. She'd received the strangest letter after news of the Story Forest's burning and rebirth had reached Thesaurus. The writing was large and loopy and in some places, barely decipherable. Some of it was babble, inky letters spooling across the parchment as if the writer's pen hadn't been able to keep up with the thoughts flowing from head to page.

She thought, however, that it mentioned something about floating letters, a plan gone awry and … was that word 'epiphany'? She wasn't exactly sure what it all meant.

However, what she *could* glean from it was this.

Her father – just as the town committee had once feared – finally wanted to meet her.

He signed off simply as 'H'.

***

The Story Forest had never felt better.

Ideas danced through its glades and copses; letters bloomed from its branches, hanging like succulent fruit. New story arcs bridged faster-flowing rivers that were lusty with red herrings and sprightly nymphs poised for tricking unwary travellers.

Tall waterfalls of words cascaded down rocky precipices nevertheless dwarfed by the towering trees of the forest. Freshly carved doors appeared in trunks – invitations that any passing adventurer surely couldn't resist. The fairies waltzed and piped their music; the animals went about their business just as they always had (though even old Bay the badger seemed to have an extra glint in his eyes these nights). The Story Forest was full to the brim with new narratives and plots, twists and turns, beginnings and endings.

Stories had always existed – in the mind, the air, on the rock and the page. New homes for stories continually emerged beyond all of these, however, and the Story Forest embraced them all.

They tasted delicious.

Indeed, even Mr Tipett's metallic tang, with its synthetic and rather sour qualities, was now freshly flavoured with a woody, nutty taste since his departure from the forest.

Freddie, of course, already had a love of adventure within him but his flavour too now had added spice of the bookish variety. Yes, he carried with him an additional minty sap-like aroma, which pleased the Story Forest very much.

And Hallow?

Well, he'd gone from being rather tasteless and mulchy – a mixture of milk on the turn, spoiled berries and rotting vegetation – to a creature who had since acquired a tantalising essence that was shaping up to be much more palatable. It was still deciding what it was going to be, but the important thing was that it existed.

The Travelling Trees received all of this news in their respective locations as the roots from the Story Forest hummed and thrummed; as the wind carried their stories. They stood strong together and story flowed through them.

Chapter Thirty-three
On with the Show

Two years later, the refurbishment of Portsteven Library was complete. In the intervening years, the library had decamped to a temporary home in the town hall, which had encouraged even more people to browse its books and see everything it had to offer, when they visited for other events in the building.

The new library, however, was a dream, with tall glossy bookshelves of polished wood and matching desks scattered throughout. Mercury had been heavily involved with designing the interior and had insisted on keeping wood, rather than installing metal bookcases, which gave the library a warm almost stately home appearance. Old cornices had been restored and a beautiful stained glass window depicting stacks of books, along with readers and fabulous adventure scenes, now adorned the front of the building. It was actually inspired by the Story Forest, though Freddie hadn't told his mum that it was actually a real place that he'd visited in the Book-Keeper world when he'd described it to her.

Bright, squishy sofas and armchairs beckoned readers to stay a while and even a couple of rocking chairs had appeared, which quite a few of the older patrons often fought over. Rich purple curtains hung at the windows and colourful artwork and bookish quotes decorated the walls. There was also an impressive new automated system for checking books in and out of the library, leaving Mercury and her fellow librarians more time to assist visitors and facilitate groups such as the Silver Surfers. Lots of new members had joined the library too, which Mercury was delighted about.

The official grand reopening of Portsteven Library took place on a sunny Saturday morning in April. The town was buzzing about who was going to cut the ribbon but no one seemed to know their identity, even Mercury. "Which is *very* unusual," she said. "I just hope it's someone interesting!"

Indeed, the only people who knew the identity of the

special guest were Freddie, Graham and Mr Tipett, who was a newly signed-up member of both the library and Freddie's book club, which now actually *was* a book club. Mr Tipett hadn't told Freddie *everything* about his time in the Story Forest, but Freddie understood that his former nemesis had journeyed deeper into its heart than any of the rest of them and, as a result, had rediscovered the pure joy of storytelling.

"Stories, Freddie," said Mr Tipett in awe. "They're what the world is made of. I'll never forget that place. Never."

Freddie finally admitted to his mother on the morning of the grand reopening that he knew who was coming along to cut the ribbon. All he would tell her, however, was that it was someone who liked space, had written books and was "into music."

"I have no idea, Freddie!" said Mercury, exasperated, and Freddie smiled a secret smile.

When they arrived at the library, there was a crowd already waiting, including photographers and reporters bustling about trying to find out who the mystery guest was. Freddie, Brain and Rob joined Gwen and Graham, with Freddie scouring the bookshelves, hoping she had come for this. At first, he saw nothing and then, a tiny door slid open and someone slipped in between the books.

Meg.

Outside, a car with tinted windows pulled up, while inside, the library hushed.

Mercury's mouth dropped open when she saw the man with his mass of silver curls stride into the library, flanked by what Freddie assumed were a couple of not so discreet bodyguards.

"Is that who I think it is?" asked Brain in awe.

"Who is it, then?" said Gwen. "I don't … Oh, wait a minute. Isn't he the guitarist from that band – who has the same surname as you, Freddie? What's it called again …? Something to do with royalty, I think."

"Yep – and it's my mum's absolute favourite," said Freddie with a grin. "Well, I had to use my fairy wish for *some*thing. Graham called in a few favours with some of his old physics professor colleagues and … a little bit of magic did the rest!"

He caught Meg's eye and winked.

Epilogue

Nobody knows where the Book-Keepers came from. Perhaps they grew out of books, like long-limbed literary children; perhaps they always existed and were just waiting for stories to bring them to life.

Or, perhaps – perhaps some kind and clever soul created them along with the very first book, to make sure all the many tales that were to be told over the years were well looked after and always found their readers.

Perhaps we will never know.

The Book-Keepers are a secretive race, and yet … They will always do whatever it takes to protect that which they hold most dear.

Books. What else?

Acknowledgements

Thanks to …
my family, friends and every bookworm who reads
my books.

Also to the Arts Council of Northern Ireland – and
in particular, Damian Smyth – for their ongoing
support of my writing.

Author's Note

In Northern Ireland, for the past number of years, our public libraries have been under the control of Libraries NI, unlike the rest of the UK, where I understand libraries are the responsibility of local councils.

For the purposes of *The Story Forest,* which is set in Northern Ireland, I created the Library Administration Body (LAB) to mirror the idea of Libraries NI, which is governed by a board made up mostly of local councillors. All board members are appointed by the Minister for Communities, with Libraries NI funded and overseen by Northern Ireland's Department of Communities.

In Freddie's world, the LAB has been infiltrated by Mr Tipett, who's trying to close Portsteven Library down. Fortunately, in our world, Libraries NI is doing a great job of looking after our public libraries – for us today and the generations to come.

PS The name 'Portsteven' is a combination of the 'Port' from Portstewart (not far from where I live) and one of my brothers' names.

About the Author

Claire Savage grew up deep in the countryside around Magherafelt and Desertmartin, Northern Ireland, where she spent lots of time exploring outdoors and, of course, reading books. Unlike Freddie, she was a bookworm from as far back as she can remember and she loved nothing better than settling down with a good story.

Over the years, Claire borrowed lots of books from her local library in Magherafelt, as well as from Portstewart Library when she was on summer holidays on the North Coast. In fact, if you're from the area then you might see  some similarities between Portsteven Library and Portstewart Library, as well as the surrounding locality …

Inspired by daily outings with her cocker spaniel, Reuben, Claire's writing is influenced a lot by the coastal landscape where she now lives.

The Story Forest is Claire's third middle-grade novel for readers aged between 8-12 years. She previously published a duology – *Magical Masquerade* (2017) and *Phantom Phantasia* (2018). *Magical Masquerade* was officially launched at the Belfast Book Festival 2017 and was also included in Derry's SBOOKY Festival and the Dublin Book Festival 2017. Both books are available online as e-books and paperbacks, as well as in-store at the Giant's Causeway Visitors' Centre.

Claire is a copywriter by day and also writes short stories

and poetry, with work published in literary journals including *The Lonely Crowd, The Incubator, The Launchpad, The Ghastling* and *SHIFT Lit - Derry*. In January 2020, she set up an organisation called Sesheta with fellow author, Kelly Creighton, receiving funding from the Arts Council of Northern Ireland's Small Grants Programme to co-edit an anthology of Christmas short stories from Northern Irish writers. Entitled *Underneath the Tree,* this was published in November 2020.

Claire has twice received General Arts Awards from the Arts Council of Northern Ireland's National Lottery Fund and was chosen as one of Lagan Online's '12NOW' (New Original Writers) in 2016/17. In November 2020 she also received a grant from the Arts Council of NI's Individuals Emergency Resilience Programme (IERP), funded by the Department for Communities, to support her ongoing work as a writer and creative professional in Northern Ireland.

Claire enjoys hosting the Giant's Causeway Book Club every month for the National Trust, which was launched in June 2018. She is currently working on her first novel for adults.

Author blog: www.clairesavagewriting.wordpress.com

Facebook: Claire Savage – Author

Twitter: @ClaireLSavage

Instagram: @clairesavage_editorial

Author photo by Moira McFadden.

Printed in Great Britain
by Amazon

56780235R00170